# Match Wits with Super Sleuth Nancy Drew!

## Collect the Original
## Nancy Drew Mystery Stories®
by Carolyn Keene

### *Available in Hardcover!*

## Celebrate 60 Years with the World's Best Detective!

# MYSTERY OF CROCODILE ISLAND

In a response to a friend's call for help, Nancy's father, a lawyer, asks her to travel to mysterious Crocodile Island with her friends Bess and George to study the reptiles and try to uncover a group of suspected poachers.

Upon their arrival in Florida, the girls are kidnapped but cleverly escape to pursue their detective work. Dangers mount as they cope with reptiles, enemy boats, and exciting chases after the men who are responsible for a sinister racket that involves many unsuspecting victims. In the end, Nancy makes a bold move to untangle the mass of clues. She and Ned become imprisoned in the enemy's submarine and are held for ransom!

How Nancy and Ned are saved and the tables turned on the owners of Crocodile Island are left for the reader to discover.

*Nancy realized that the child would be bashed against the jagged breakwater!*

NANCY DREW MYSTERY STORIES®

# Mystery of
# Crocodile Island

## BY CAROLYN KEENE

GROSSET & DUNLAP
Publishers • New York
A member of The Putnam & Grosset Group

PRINTED ON RECYCLED PAPER

Copyright © 1978 by Simon & Schuster, Inc. All rights reserved.
Published by Grosset & Dunlap, Inc., a member of The Putnam &
Grosset Group, New York. Published simultaneously in Canada. Printed in the U.S.A.
NANCY DREW MYSTERY STORIES® is a registered trademark of Simon & Schuster,
Inc. GROSSET & DUNLAP is a trademark of Grosset & Dunlap, Inc.
Library of Congress Catalog Card Number: 77-76128 ISBN 0-448-09555-6
2003 Printing

## Contents

| CHAPTER | | PAGE |
|---|---|---|
| I | A RISKY ADVENTURE | 1 |
| II | NEW NAMES | 9 |
| III | ESCAPE | 18 |
| IV | CROCODILE FARM | 30 |
| V | A THREAT | 38 |
| VI | THE IMPOSTOR | 48 |
| VII | SEA DETECTIVES | 58 |
| VIII | INDIAN TRICKS | 66 |
| IX | HURRICANE LEGEND | 75 |
| X | THE RUNAWAY'S CLUES | 83 |
| XI | AN IDENTIFICATION | 90 |
| XII | CHILD IN DANGER | 100 |
| XIII | DOUBLOONS! | 109 |
| XIV | PERISCOPE PURSUIT | 118 |
| XV | JUNGLE ATTACK | 126 |
| XVI | EXCITING PHONE CALL | 135 |
| XVII | DEADLY GOLF BALL | 144 |
| XVIII | SNAKES | 153 |
| XIX | TRIPLE SLEUTHING | 162 |
| XX | SUBMARINE PRISONERS | 171 |

*Mystery of Crocodile Island*

# CHAPTER I

## A Risky Adventure

NANCY Drew and her friend Bess Marvin were seated in the Drew living room, eagerly awaiting the arrival of Nancy's father.

"I wish your dad would hurry and get here," Bess said impatiently. "Nancy, have you any idea what the trip he wants us to take is all about?"

The attractive eighteen-year-old strawberry blond shook her head. "I know the place, but not the mystery we're to solve."

"Where is the place?" Bess asked.

"Florida. Dad didn't tell me what part, though."

Bess giggled. "Any part will be all right with me, as long as there's warm weather and swimming."

Nancy smiled. "Probably all of us will be glad to swim. At this time of year it can get pretty hot down there."

A ring at the front door interrupted her. Nancy hurried to answer it. The visitor was Bess's cousin George Fayne. George was a vivacious dark-haired girl with a winning smile and a great appetite for adventure. She and Bess had helped Nancy with many mysteries.

"Hi, George!" Nancy greeted her friend. "Come in."

When the two walked into the living room, Bess pointed to a shoe box George carried. "What's in there?" she inquired.

George's eyes twinkled. She took off the lid, which had several small holes punched in it. "You can see," she said, "but don't touch."

In the box lay a twelve inch baby crocodile. Since it did not move, the girls assumed it was asleep. George held up the box and tapped the underside. At once the crocodile began to wiggle! It opened its jaws wide and swished its tail.

Bess screamed. "Put the lid on and get that thing out of here!" she demanded.

George laughed. "It's not real! Nancy, your dad asked me to stop at the River Heights Trick Shop and buy a rubber crocodile. He didn't explain why."

She replaced the lid and set the box on the table. "The clerk in the store said if you tickle the trick crocodile, it will wiggle. It's meant to scare people, but it can't possibly hurt you."

Bess looked doubtful, and George went on,

*"Get that thing out of here!"* Bess demanded.

ʰ"If this reptile were real, the government would take it and fine me twenty thousand dollars."

"What!" Bess cried out. "That's incredible."

"Or I could spend five years in jail for possessing it without government permission."

"But why?" Bess asked.

"Because crocodiles are a vanishing species," Nancy put in. "There used to be plenty of them in this country, but now there are only a few left in Florida."

Bess's eyes opened wide. "Do you think your father is going to send us to the part where there are crocodiles?"

Nancy was looking out the window. "We'll soon know," she replied. "He's driving in now."

Carson Drew, a leading attorney in River Heights, parked his car in the garage, then came into the house by way of the kitchen. When he reached the living room, he kissed Nancy and greeted the other two girls.

"Don't keep us in suspense any longer," Nancy pleaded. "Are we going to crocodile land?"

Her tall, handsome father sat down on the couch. "In a way, yes. This is the story. An old college friend of mine named Roger Gonzales lives in Key Biscayne outside of Miami. Biscayne Bay is full of small islands, which are called keys. Most of them are inhabited, but some of the smaller ones are like jungles and nobody lives on them. Some twenty miles from Key Biscayne there's a key that has been nicknamed Crocodile Island. A group of men operate a crocodile farm on it. They breed these reptiles to sell to zoos or other places where sightseers can view them."

As Mr. Drew paused, Bess spoke, with fright in her voice. "And you're going to ask us to go to this alligator farm?"

Mr. Drew smiled. "Crocodile farm, Bess. There's a difference."

"There is?"

"Yes. The American alligator has a much broader snout than the crocodile, and is less vicious and active. The two reptiles are about equal in size and can grow up to twelve feet in length, but the croc weighs about a third less than the 'gator."

Bess shivered. "I don't want to meet either one."

George laughed. To tease Bess, she said, "Mr. Drew, tell us some more scary things about crocodiles."

Bess groaned.

"They like to live in large bodies of shallow salty water," Mr. Drew continued, "preferably in sluggish rivers, open swamps, and marshes that are brackish. They raise their heads when you go near them and—"

"Oh, stop!" Bess begged.

Mr. Drew grinned. "But I'm not finished. In this country crocs were formerly found around the southernmost tip of Florida, but because so many people went to live on Key Biscayne, the crocs moved into the Everglades. They have webbed feet and can walk on soft ground."

"How fast can they run?" George asked.

"Very fast. Like horses!"

"Forget it!" Bess declared. "I'm staying home. Who wants to be eaten?"

"American crocodiles occasionally do attack animals and people," Mr. Drew admitted. "A croc can twist a large animal to pieces by seizing one part of it, then turning rapidly in the water."

George grimaced. "I think I agree with Bess!"

"Don't worry," Mr. Drew said. "You probably won't meet any wild crocs. What I'm talking about is a farm where they're bred in captivity. There's a mystery connected with the place that I hope you girls can solve."

"What kind of mystery?" George asked.

"I'll tell you in a minute." Mr. Drew looked at the shoe box. "I see you did the errand, George. Thank you very much. I thought you girls might want to study a rubber crocodile to get acquainted with its looks."

He rose and walked over to the table and removed the lid. George suggested that he lift the box and tap the bottom. He did, and once more the baby crocodile wiggled its tail and opened and closed its jaws.

"This is certainly a good imitation," Mr. Drew

remarked. He sat down again and went on with his story. "Mr. Gonzales has stock in the crocodile farm, which is called Crocodile Ecology Company. He doesn't live or work there, however. He's a silent partner, so to speak.

"Recently he has become suspicious that the business arrangements on the island are not what they should be, and that his partners are up to something dishonest."

Nancy asked, "And this Mr. Gonzales has requested that we investigate Crocodile Island?"

"That's right," her father replied. "However, he doesn't want his partners to know it, so you girls are not to visit his home or his office, or even phone him. Roger Gonzales is afraid his partners are spying on him, and in some way may find out he's starting an investigation."

Mr. Drew told the girls they should pretend to be just tourists. "I'd even suggest that while you're there you act like silly young girls, so that the Crocodile Ecology people won't catch on. The last thing you want them to know is that you all have high detective IQ's."

Bess laughed. "That'll be easy enough for me. I can act silly any time, but Nancy will really have to play the part."

Mr. Drew asked to be excused. "I must get back to my office for another case."

After he had gone, the telephone rang and Nancy hurried to answer it in the hall.

"Is this the Drew home?" a man's voice asked.

"Yes. Who is this?"

"The River Heights Trick Shop. I want to speak to the girl who bought the crocodile."

Nancy motioned to George and handed her the receiver.

"Hello?" George said.

"Are you the girl who bought the crocodile?"

"Yes. Why?"

"You're in great danger!" the man told her. "The boy who was working here gave you a live one by mistake."

"What!" George cried out.

"Bring it back right away," the man ordered. "If you don't, the police will arrest you!"

George was aghast. She could be put in jail for five years or be fined twenty thousand dollars!

Nancy, who had overheard the conversation, looked toward the box on the table. Her father had not bothered to put the lid on after examining the crocodile. Now the reptile was climbing out of the container!

It opened its jaws wide. Though the crocodile was only a baby, there was no doubt about its viciousness. It could easily snap off someone's finger!

Just then the other girls in the room noticed that the crocodile had escaped from its container. As Nancy dashed toward it, George froze and Bess screamed in fear!

# CHAPTER II

## New Names

MRS. Hannah Gruen, the Drews' housekeeper, heard the commotion and rushed in from the kitchen. By now the baby crocodile lay at the edge of the table, making low hissing sounds.

Hannah backed away in alarm, even though she usually had plenty of courage when confronted with a crisis. A middle-aged woman, she had brought Nancy up after Mrs. Drew's death, when Nancy was three years old. Since then kindly Mrs. Gruen had fostered the girl's natural instinct to face danger without flinching.

"Wh—what on earth is going on here?" Hannah asked.

Before anyone could answer, Nancy's bullterrier Togo slipped into the room behind the housekeeper. As soon as he spied the little reptile, he began to bark wildly. He jumped up in the air, trying to reach the crocodile with his paws.

"Don't hurt it!" Nancy exclaimed. She grabbed Togo by his collar and tried to keep him from nipping the little creature.

"I'll take Togo," Hannah offered.

Nancy walked up to the table and turned the shoe carton on its end. Then, with the lid, she gently pushed the crocodile back toward it. Apparently the dog's barking and yapping had frightened it, and the little reptile willingly crawled into the box.

"Thank goodness!" Hannah Gruen said with a sigh of relief as Nancy put the lid back on.

"I'm glad that's over!" Bess added. "If one little baby can scare us like that, what'll we do when we get to a farm full of great big crocs?"

Mrs. Gruen laughed. "No doubt the reptiles are kept in pits and can't get out," she said. "Don't worry, Bess."

Togo continued to bark and jump, so Nancy led him outside and put him in his run. The dog had helped her many times in her detective work, which had started with *The Secret of the Old Clock*. Recently she had unraveled *The Strange Message in the Parchment*.

Meanwhile, Hannah had found a sturdy cord to secure the shoe box. When Nancy returned to the living room, she suggested that the three girls go downtown and deliver the baby crocodile to its owner.

"I second the motion," Bess said. "The sooner we get this creature out of here, the better I'll like it!"

When they reached the store, Bess stayed in the car, while Nancy and George went inside the shop. The owner, Noly Reareck, greeted the girls with a look of relief.

"You have no idea what a load you've taken off my mind," he said. "You see, I have a license to keep Crocky as a pet and have agreed to keep it in suitable surroundings and never to abuse it, kill it, or sell its hide."

Mr. Reareck explained that it was unfortunate the little reptile had been sold to George. "I had to go to the post office," he said, "and asked a neighborhood boy to watch the shop for a few minutes. He decided to play a joke on me. Instead of selling you a rubber crocodile that can be made to wiggle and open its mouth, he gave you my pet. It's a good thing you told him it was for Carson Drew, or I wouldn't have been able to trace it. I'm mighty relieved that Crocky didn't bite anyone."

Bess, who was waiting in the car, wondered why the girls did not come back and walked into the shop. George explained about the switching of the crocodiles, then Nancy asked Mr. Reareck where the young reptile had come from.

"Crocodile Island in Florida," he said.

The girls looked at one another in amazement.

"Crocodile Island?" Bess blurted out. "Why, that's where—"

She stopped suddenly because George stepped on her toes. Nancy was relieved. If Mr. Reareck had any connection with Crocodile Island, she did not want him to know about the girls' mission.

The three thanked the shop owner and left. Nancy dropped Bess and George off at their homes, then returned to her own house. With Hannah Gruen looking on and offering advice from time to time, Nancy chose a wardrobe to take on the trip. Among her summer clothes were two bathing suits, a terry-cloth beach robe, and a jump suit.

After she finished packing, Nancy learned from Hannah that her father had come home. She went into his room, where he was reading.

"Dad," she said, "Mr. Reareck told us that he got his pet from Crocodile Island. It would be a good idea if you could find out if he has any connection with the Crocodile Ecology Company other than just having bought Crocky."

Her father promised to do so. "I'm glad you told me."

The next day Nancy and her friends climbed into a plane bound for New York, where they would change for a nonstop flight to Miami. After they landed in New York, the girls hurried into the huge airport building and up to a counter to arrange for seats on their jet to Florida.

The clerk smiled at Nancy and said, "You are Miss Nancy Drew?"

"Yes, I am."

"We received a message that you are to get in touch with your father at once. It's possible your trip will be canceled."

Puzzled, Nancy hurried to a phone and was soon talking to Mr. Drew. "Is something wrong, Dad?" she asked, worried.

The lawyer replied that his friend Roger Gonzales had called him to say that his suspicions about the Crocodile Ecology Company had been unfounded. "He told me there is no need for legal or protective action," Mr. Drew explained, "and he has canceled your motel reservations."

Nancy was stunned by the news, but before she could express her dismay, Mr. Drew went on, "I'm afraid that Roger was forced to make that call, and needs help. That's why you should go ahead with your trip. But don't get in touch with him until you hear from me.

"I have arranged for you to stay at the home of friends of mine, named Mr. and Mrs. Henry Cosgrove in Key Biscayne. They have a sixteen-year-old son, Danny, who's an excellent sailor and familiar with the keys. He can take you around in their motorboat. I'm sure he'll be of great help to you in your sleuthing."

"Oh, good," Nancy said. "I'm glad we don't have to give up the trip."

Mr. Drew urged his daughter and her friends to be very careful.

"We will," Nancy promised, then asked, "Have you had a chance to speak to Mr. Reareck?"

"Yes. He saw an ad in the paper about the Crocodile Ecology Farm and wrote to them, ordering the pet. He doesn't know the partners or anything about them. Well, good-by, dear, and have a great time."

When Nancy joined Bess and George, they were worried about the turn of events.

"Do you suppose," Bess asked, "that somehow the people on Crocodile Island found out that we were coming, and that you're an amateur detective, Nancy?"

"That's possible," Nancy replied. "Anyway, since Dad wants us to go ahead, let's get our seat numbers."

The girls did, then went to the lounge and settled on three seats away from other waiting passengers to discuss what they would do when they reached Key Biscayne.

George said, "Perhaps we should disguise ourselves with wigs and quick-tanning lotions. Bess could become a brunette, I could be a blond, and Nancy a gray-haired old lady."

"Thanks." Nancy laughed. "It would be fun,

but the suspects on Crocodile Island have never seen us before. What good would a disguise be?"

After a few moments' thought, Bess spoke up. "You're right, they haven't seen us. But they evidently know who we are. Do you think it would be safer if we changed our names? We could use pseudonyms when necessary."

"What names do you suggest?" George asked.

Nancy smiled. "Suppose I call myself Anne, and Bess can be Elizabeth, and George—"

Quickly George interrupted her. "Not Georgia!" she exclaimed.

Bess laughed. Georgia was her cousin's real name, but she would never allow anyone to call her by it.

"I'll be Jackie," George declared.

The girls discussed a last name and finally decided on Boonton, which was Mrs. Marvin's maiden name.

Nancy looked at her watch. "I'll have time to phone Dad and tell him our new names. He can inform Mr. Gonzales."

When she returned, George said, "Okay, Anne. Our section of seats has been called to board. Let's go!"

Bess grinned. "Oh, Jackie, dear," she said, "You have such brilliant ideas!"

The girls entered the giant airliner in a happy mood, and sat down side by side. During the flight they teased one another, using their assumed names. They passed part of the time reading magazines and eating a delicious lunch.

In the middle of the afternoon they arrived in Miami and went to the baggage-claim area. As they retrieved their suitcases, a young man walked up to them.

"Pardon me," he said, "but are you the girls who are visiting the Cosgroves?"

"That's right," George said. "And you?"

"My name is Steven. They sent me to drive you to their house. We'll get a porter and have him bring your bags."

Steven led them to a beautiful gold-colored car.

"Does this belong to the Cosgroves?" Nancy asked.

"No, it's mine," he said and opened the doors for them.

"It's yummy," Bess remarked and plopped into the cream-colored, velvety back seat. George climbed in next to her, while Nancy rode in front with Steven.

On the way the girls admired the sprawling, large homes and the glistening bay. Steven, who was not very talkative, answered their questions merely with a yes or no, so after a while they gave up including him in their conversation.

He drove over the causeway and through Key Biscayne. At last they came to an area of beautiful homes that occupied large pieces of property.

Steven turned into a long driveway and approached an elegant mansion. He stopped at the front door and offered to carry the bags up to the girls' rooms.

Nancy rang the bell. The door was opened by a middle-aged couple.

"You must be Nancy Drew," the woman said. She was cordial but did not smile. "And these are your friends, Bess and George."

Nancy nodded and asked, "And you are Mr. and Mrs. Cosgrove?"

"Yes," the man replied. He did not smile either, and the girls felt uncomfortable at the cool welcome.

The couple silently escorted them to the second floor and showed each visitor to a large and expensively furnished bedroom. Steven followed with their luggage.

Nancy walked to the picture window at the far end of her room to gaze down into the beautiful garden. Bess and George also looked out their windows. None of them had noticed that their hosts had silently closed the doors to the hall.

When the three friends tried to get together before joining the Cosgroves downstairs, they found that they had been locked in!

# CHAPTER III

## *Escape*

ALTHOUGH Nancy felt a tight knot of alarm in the pit of her stomach, her mind was racing. Obviously she and her friends had been kidnapped, and what made it worse was that the three girls were locked in separate rooms! No chance to plan an escape!

Before the young sleuth could decide what to do, she heard Bess cry out, "Anne, Jackie, where are you?"

"Locked in, just like you," George's voice came faintly.

"This is awful!" Bess wailed. "What'll we do?"

"Don't panic," Nancy advised. "That won't get us anywhere."

The girls realized that if they tried to discuss a plan of action through the walls, their captors would hear them and foil any attempted escape. Each one had to fend for herself!

While Bess and George began a minute examination of their prisons, Nancy looked through the keyhole. The key was gone, but she was sure the lock on this bedroom door was a common type.

"That's a break," she thought and opened her purse.

She took out a bobby pin and a nail file. First she inserted the file into the keyhole and held it tight. Next she pushed in the bobby pin. By manipulating first one, then the other, she finally managed to get the door open.

Silently Nancy stepped into the hallway and listened. She heard the front door slam, and tiptoed to a window just in time to see the sham Cosgroves get into a green sedan and roar out of the driveway.

Obviously Steven had left too, because his fancy gold-colored car was nowhere in sight. All was quiet, and Nancy was inclined to think they were alone in the house. But she could not be sure.

Quickly she went to Bess's door and started to work with her makeshift tools. Bess heard the noise. "Nancy? George?" she called.

"Shhh!" Nancy whispered. "I'm trying to get you out."

Within minutes she had released the lock and entered the room.

"You're a doll, Nancy Drew," Bess cried out, hugging her friend in relief. "Have you any idea where we are? This is a pretty grand-looking place. I can't imagine that the kind of people who live here would imprison us in their own house!"

"I can't either," Nancy replied. "I have a strong hunch that our captors borrowed this place. By the way, I saw those people leave. But they could come back any minute. Let's work on George's door!"

The girls quickly went to their friend's room and again Nancy inserted her nail file into the lock. There was no sound from inside the room. Had something happened to George? Finally the bolt snapped and Bess pushed the door open. The room was empty!

"George!" Nancy called out softly. There was no reply.

"Oh, dear," Bess said. "Maybe those people took her out of here!"

"I doubt it," Nancy reasoned. "We would have heard the commotion. Besides, we spoke to her just a few minutes ago." She walked to the window, and a big grin spread over her face.

"Bess, come here!" she said, pointing to a large maple tree directly in front of her. A long branch extended almost to the window. Climbing down the last two feet of the trunk was George!

"Hi!" Nancy called softly.

George looked up and chuckled. "I'm an escapee!"

Nancy smiled as Bess reached her side and heaved a sigh of relief. George continued her descent. "Bess, do you want to come down the way I did? Or use the stairs? And how did you two get loose?" she queried.

Bess made a face, then smiled. "Nancy is a great lock picker."

"Shh!" Nancy warned. "We don't know for sure that everyone's gone. Somebody could have been left to guard us!"

"So what do we do next?" Bess asked.

"I think you and I can risk tiptoeing through the house," Nancy replied. "Quick! Grab your bag. I'll get George's and mine. We'll meet her outside."

She motioned to the girl below to wait for them and the two quickly got their luggage. They hurried down the stairs, trying to move as noiselessly as possible. They opened the front door and slipped outside. George was waiting for them.

"I don't think we should take the road," Nancy said. "The kidnappers could come back. Let's walk through the backyard and see if we can get help at one of those houses in the distance."

The girls had not gone far when they realized that the ground beyond the garden was marshy. The mud ruined their shoes and spattered their dresses, but the three friends hurried on until they were out of range of the house.

Bess stopped and put down her bag. "My arm

is killing me," she said. "Can't we rest a minute?"

Nancy looked back. The house behind them seemed deserted. "I guess we're safe enough," she decided, so she and George dropped their heavy suitcases.

"Boy, what an experience!" George said. "Our kidnappers must have overheard Mr. Gonzales's call to your father, Nancy, when he asked for help."

Nancy nodded. "And the second call, when Mr. Gonzales canceled our reservations must have been made from another phone," she said thoughtfully, "otherwise they wouldn't have sent Steven to the airport to get us."

"Who do you think our kidnappers are?" Bess asked.

"They must be connected with the Crocodile Ecology Company," Nancy replied.

"I wonder if they own that house." George said.

"I doubt it. They wouldn't be foolish enough to imprison us in their own home. If we got away, it would be too easy to trace them."

Bess giggled. "They were foolish to leave us alone."

"I think we should hurry on," George said. "If they come back and find we're gone, they're bound to look for us."

The girls picked up their bags and trudged through the swamp until they reached the house they had seen ahead of them. As they went up to the front porch, Bess looked down at her dress and shoes. "We're absolute sights," she said. "What will the people think when they see us?"

"That we're swamp ducks," George quipped.

The girls rang the bell. There was no answer. Nancy knocked, but no one seemed to be home.

"What are we going to do?" Bess asked, worried. "We can't go on like this! And there's not another house in sight!"

They left their suitcases on the porch and walked around to the back. Luckily, there was a wall telephone on a rear patio. Nancy called the operator and asked to speak to the police department. When a sergeant answered, she explained the girls' predicament and asked if someone could come and help them.

"Right away, miss," he replied, and within ten minutes a squad car pulled up with two officers in it.

One jumped out and walked up to them. "You say you were kidnapped and escaped?" he said.

"That's right," Nancy told him and explained exactly what had happened. "We're on our way to visit Mr. and Mrs. Henry Cosgrove, but we don't know how to find the place."

"I'll order a cab for you," the officer said, and asked his companion to make the call. "I know the Cosgroves," he continued. "It's a long ride from here."

He took a notebook from his pocket and wrote down the circumstances of the kidnapping. First he requested the names and addresses of the girls. This time Nancy gave him the correct ones. She described Steven, the young man who had met them at the airport, as well as the couple who had locked them into the bedrooms.

"We'll get to work on the case at once," the officer promised.

He walked to the squad car and picked up his radio phone. First he asked that a taxi be sent out, then gave a full report on the case. When he returned to the girls, he said, "A cab will be here in a few minutes. Is this your first visit to Key Biscayne?"

When the three nodded yes, he shook his head. "I'm sorry your introduction to our town was so disastrous. Believe me, you'll find that Key Biscayne is a mighty nice area. Well, I hope you'll have an enjoyable time while you're here."

In a few minutes a taxi pulled up in front of the house. The driver looked at the girls curiously.

Bess explained they had walked through the swamp after coming from the wrong direction to the Cosgroves' home. She gave the correct address and they set off.

Unlike the couple who tried to kidnap them, Helen and Henry Cosgrove were delightful. Nancy quickly explained why they were so unkempt.

"What a dreadful experience!" Mrs. Cosgrove exclaimed. "We must report it to the police at once!"

"I've already done that," Nancy said, and told the whole story.

Mr. Cosgrove said, "I got to the airport late because our car wouldn't start. When I arrived, you had already gone. I thought you might have taken a taxi and come back home. We started to worry when you didn't arrive. I even called your home in River Heights, but no one was there."

"Good," Nancy said with a chuckle. "Dad and Hannah didn't have a chance to become alarmed."

At this point a sixteen-year-old boy with red hair and twinkling eyes walked in and was introduced to the girls as Danny Cosgrove. He looked at their dirty shoes and clothes and said, "I guess you got here the hard way. What happened?"

Nancy told him and he responded, "Your dad said you would be here to solve a mystery and there might be some danger connected with it. You sure made a good start!"

The girls laughed, then asked to be excused to change their clothes. Mrs. Cosgrove led them to two bedrooms. "Who wants to share the big one?" she asked.

Bess and George said they would, so Nancy took the smaller room.

During dinner Nancy explained more about

the mystery, but asked the Cosgroves to keep it a secret. "We decided to use fake names to avoid detection by any suspects," Nancy said. "But now I'm not so sure it's worth it."

Mrs. Cosgrove spoke. "I'd try it if I were you. Even if part of this group you're about to investigate knows who you are, not everyone connected with the Crocodile Ecology Company has seen you. By using fictitious names, you can probably fool them."

"What are your new names?" Danny asked.

"I'm Anne," said Nancy.

"And I'm Elizabeth," Bess replied.

George grinned. "I'm Jackie."

Nancy's first bit of detective work was to call the police early next morning. She inquired about the house where they had been imprisoned and was told that the owners were away on vacation.

The girls' kidnappers had broken in and "borrowed" the premises for their scheme. The police managed to track down Steven, who told them the couple had approached him in a supermarket and asked him if he would like to earn some money. They needed someone to pick up three visitors from the airport and bring them to their house.

"Steven agreed and assured us he knew nothing about a kidnapping," the officer concluded. "We're inclined to believe his story, but we'll keep an eye on him."

After Nancy had put down the phone, Mr. Cosgrove asked the girls if they would like Danny to take them to Crocodile Island in the family's motorized skiff.

"It's high tide now and a good time to go," he said. "I wish you luck in your sleuthing," he added, smiling.

"Thank you very much," Nancy said. "Do you think we'll have a chance to go on the island?"

"Sometimes they do allow visitors," Mr. Cosgrove explained. "On certain days of the week, but I don't know about today. You'll have to see."

The four walked to the marina where the boat was kept.

"How do you like the name I gave it?" Danny asked.

The girls laughed when they saw what was painted on the side of the skiff.

*"Pirate!"* George exclaimed. "Even if you hadn't told me, I'd have known a boy picked it."

"Do you go after all the treasure that's supposed to be buried on these islands?" Bess asked him.

"I sure do," Danny replied. "The trouble is, some of the small keys floated away in hurricanes and any treasure on them is lost forever."

"What a shame!" George teased. "And here we came all the way to Florida, thinking we could dig up a million doubloons!"

The young people laughed, then stepped

aboard the skiff. Four swivel chairs were bolted
to the deck, and Danny explained that this made
it easy for fishermen to turn in all directions.
Then he pointed to the large outboard motor in
the rear of the craft. "It weighs two hundred and
fifty pounds and is raised and lowered hydrauli-
cally."

"Why do you have to raise it?" Bess asked.

"When you get caught in low tide, you literally
have to jump along over the sand dunes at a very
fast clip. If you don't, you're apt to get stuck."

Danny settled himself behind the wheel and
started the boat. As they rode along, he pointed
out the shoreline of Key Biscayne with its high-
rise condominiums and many-storied hotels. But
soon they left the area and one little island after
another came into view.

"All of these were built up by coral formations
and mangrove trees," Danny explained. "I'll
show you some trees along the edge. The way they
grow is fascinating."

He pulled up to a small key and stopped the
boat. The narrow mangrove trunks rose some
fifteen feet into the air, then started to bend over.
Their branches were heavy with leaves, which in
turn hung down into the water. Being thick and
close together, they were a natural catchall for
whatever floated by, and together they formed a
solid shoreline.

"Over there," said Danny, pointing, "is a place

where the water is a little deeper. We can glide in between two of the wide-spreading trees and you can get a better look."

He raised the outboard motor somewhat, moved the skiff forward, then headed among the mangroves. It was a strange sight. Roots twisted and turned. Among them and beyond the shoreline lay fragments of weathered coral rock.

Suddenly there was a grinding sound under the skiff, which stopped so abruptly it almost threw the girls into the water!

# CHAPTER IV

## Crocodile Farm

"WHAT did we hit?" Bess cried out. "Oh, I hope it didn't ram a hole in the skiff!"

"I doubt it," Danny replied. From the deck he picked up a long pole with a pronged hook on the end. Leaning over the side, he poked around under the boat and raised an enormous pile of matted mangrove roots and leaves. With a chuckle, he swung it into the skiff.

"Ugh!" Bess cried out. "What are all those crawly things in there?"

"Crocodile food," Danny said and handed her a tin can. "Pick them up and drop them in this."

George laughed. "You asked the wrong person, Danny. Bess hates that kind of thing."

"You bet I do," Bess said, pulling her knees up to her chin.

Nancy took the can and she and George

scooped up the small marine creatures. Some of them were no longer than a half inch.

Nancy remarked, "A crocodile would have to eat a million of these to get even half a meal."

"That would do for a snack," Danny agreed. Then he made sure the outboard motor was not clogged.

Fortunately the green mass had come up in one big lump, and he was able to back the skiff away from the key. George threw the leaves and roots far out and once more the boat headed for Crocodile Island. The water was very shallow, and sand dunes stuck up here and there. Once in a while the skiff ran through an area where the water was dark green in color.

"These channels run quite deep," Danny explained. "Larger craft can travel only in these, whereas a flat-bottomed boat like ours can go anywhere on the bay."

A few minutes later he pointed to their left, where series of tall, stout poles protruded from the water. Many had small cottages on top.

"I've never seen anything like this before," Bess stated. "Are they summer homes?"

Danny nodded. "Right. They're weekend retreats. The owners like to get away from the city. Out here there are a lot of interesting things to see, and many birds. But not noise except from the boat motors."

"What about the poles with nothing on top?" George asked.

"The houses they supported were blown away in hurricanes," Danny explained.

Bess shivered. "I'd run at the first sign of a breeze if I lived in one of them."

Danny laughed. "I'm sure people don't stay and wait for the storm."

An hour later he reached another key. It was surrounded by a line of mangroves. As they drew closer, the girls saw stakes driven into the water, forming a fence. It stretched as far as they could see. Here and there warning signs were posted:

CROCODILE FARM
NO TRESPASSING UNDER PENALTY OF THE LAW

"So this is Crocodile Island," George remarked.

Just then Nancy noticed two bright spots in the water behind the fence. "What are those?" she asked.

"Crocodile eyes," Danny told her. "You see, these reptiles can stay completely under water except for their eyes, which are raised high in their heads. Watch!" He picked up the can of little marine creatures and tossed them toward the crocodile. Its great jaws rose and took in the food. Then the reptile swam away lazily.

Bess, who had drawn her feet back on deck, said, "I see now why the owners put up this fence. They left enough water between it and the island so the crocodiles can enjoy themselves."

Danny told her that this was the first time he had ever seen one of the creatures in this spot. "Usually they're kept in pits and guarded carefully," he added.

"Where's the entrance to the island?" Nancy questioned.

"On the far side of the key. You girls are lucky. Today is a visiting day."

There were several boats with tourists waiting to see Crocodile Island. A boardwalk ran from a small dock up through mangrove trees to a partially open area. Here, among the mangrove trees, were shallow pits fenced in with five-foot concrete walls.

Fresh sea water flowed into them through pipes. There was an elevated area in each pit so the reptiles could stay either in or out of the water.

A small Irish terrier ran around, barking loudly at the visitors.

"His name is E-fee," Danny explained. "I know because I've been here before."

"E-fee?" Bess asked. "That's a strange name."

"It's Seminole for 'dog,' " Danny said. "He has six toes on one front paw and likes to be the center of attention. He's always around on visiting days." The boy petted the little animal and E-fee licked his fingers.

A guide asked the group to follow him, and told them about the crocodiles. "The youngest ones have a greenish cast with black markings," he said. "The half-grown ones are olive green, and the senior citizens are all gray."

They came to an enclosure with a fifteen-foot-long giant in it. "This old fellow has to stay by himself," the guide said. "He doesn't seem to get along with the others. Does anyone have any questions?"

Danny spoke up. "I've heard that crocodiles can drown. Is that true?"

"It sure is," the guide replied. "Both alligators and crocodiles can stay under water until the oxygen in their lungs is used up—alligators longer than crocodiles. But finally they both have to surface."

"How often do they have to come up?" George asked.

"Oh, I'd say the crocs come up about once every hour. It depends on the water temperature. The warmer the water, the more often they have to breathe. In cold water they can hibernate a lot longer."

"Do they have to surface to eat?" a man inquired.

"Yes. They can seize their prey underwater, because they have valves in the backs of their throats that close when they open their mouths and the water can't flow into their lungs. But they have to stick their heads out to swallow."

The group walked on, and Nancy asked the guide, "What do you do with all these crocodiles?"

"The Ecology Company sells them to various zoos and parks and even to the government," he replied.

"The government?" George repeated. "What would Uncle Sam do with a lot of crocodiles?"

The guide told her they were distributed to certain areas. "You have probably heard that the crocodile is a vanishing species. We are trying to do our part in seeing that American crocodiles do not become extinct."

At this remark Bess heaved a great sigh. "Would America really be badly off if it didn't have any?"

The guide looked at her with contempt in his eyes. "Young lady, if you knew anything about ecology, you would realize how useful they are!"

Bess had no chance to reply because a loud bell rang.

"This is an alarm!" the guide exclaimed. "I must ask you all to get back to the dock as quickly as possible and leave the island!"

"Why?" Nancy asked, disappointed. "Does it mean a crocodile is loose?"

"It could be," the guide replied. "Now please, ladies and gentlemen, return to your boats without delay!"

The tourists ran. Bess was one of the first, and the others, for once, had trouble keeping up with her. Just before they reached the skiff, a guard at the dock asked them if they had registered when they came in.

"No, we forgot," Danny said. "I'll do it now." He hurried into a small office building and signed his name. Then he entered the girls' names as Anne, Elizabeth, and Jackie Boonton.

When he came out again, they had already climbed into the skiff. A man in overalls approached the *Pirate*, pulled out a camera, and snapped their pictures, then hurried away and disappeared among the mangrove trees.

Danny jumped into the skiff and pushed off. "Why was that guy taking your pictures?" he asked.

Nancy looked concerned. "I have no idea. He did it so fast we didn't have time to turn our backs or refuse."

"He didn't photograph any of the other visitors," George stated. "He singled us out—for a reason!"

Nancy nodded. "I'm sure the top men here realize who we are. Perhaps they wanted our picture to distribute to the members of the gang who haven't seen us yet!"

George frowned. "This could mean we'll be harassed by all kinds of people, wherever we go. I'm worried."

"So am I," Bess added. "I think we should return to River Heights and get out of this whole dangerous mess!"

"You don't mean that!" Nancy exclaimed.

"Yes. I do!"

Nancy and George looked at the frightened girl. Finally Nancy said, "If that's what you want to do, Bess, go ahead. As for me, I'm staying right here and seeing this mystery through!"

"So am I," George added.

There was silence for several minutes, then Bess gave in. "You know perfectly well that I wouldn't run out on my friends. But I warn you to be careful. I know I'm not as brave as you are. I hate to get hurt!"

# CHAPTER V

## *A Threat*

DANNY and the girls moved away from Crocodile Island. All of them watched anxiously to see if they were being followed.

Other tourists were leaving in their motorboats. Nancy wondered if one of them might contain a spy from the Ecology Company, sent out to pursue the *Pirate*.

"I hope not," the girl detective thought.

Nancy observed through binoculars what directions the various craft took. One seemed to stalk the *Pirate*, and Nancy had an uneasy feeling about it.

"Do you see anything?" Bess wanted to know.

"There's a fast motorboat called *The Whisper*," Nancy replied. "It seems to be tailing us."

"Is that unusual?" George asked. "After all, other people might be heading for Key Biscayne."

"Of course," Nancy answered. "It's just that

most of the boats have scattered. This one stays right in the wake of our boat."

"Oh, oh," Danny murmured. "Maybe they want to find out where we're headed. On the other hand, they wouldn't really have to bother. Anyone can check the boat registry to see who owns the *Pirate* and where we live."

"That's great," George said. "They already know who we are, and now they can find out where we're staying!"

Bess became alarmed. "Let's head for home!" she begged.

Danny looked at Nancy. "What do you say?"

"I'm not ready to leave Crocodile Island just yet. Let's go around it and see what's on the other side. We might pick up a clue."

Danny nodded. "Sure. We may even find out if a loose crocodile caused the alarm."

"What else would?" George asked.

"You girls. Someone might have recognized not Anne, Elizabeth, and Jackie, but Nancy, Bess, and George, and wanted you off the premises."

Nancy agreed that it was a possibility. "We're getting to be notorious." She chuckled.

Danny followed the shoreline of the key. *The Whisper* stayed right behind them, and soon there was no doubt in the girls' minds that the boat was pursuing them. The fast craft finally pulled alongside the *Pirate*.

With some apprehension the young people

watched the two men on *The Whisper's* deck. Both had swarthy complexions and unpleasant faces. One of them shouted, "Get away from this island!"

"Why?" Danny asked innocently.

"Because it's private property!"

"The water isn't!" George pointed out. "Besides, we're not doing any harm!"

"We don't want you here," the man insisted and shook his fist. "Now get lost!"

"Who are you?" Danny asked. "And why should we listen to you?"

"It's none of your business who we are. And if you don't listen, you'll be in trouble!"

Danny paid no attention to the warning. Instead, he revved up his engine and pulled away from the other craft. Obviously the two men did not know what to do next, so they followed the young people around the island.

Bess had scanned the shoreline through binoculars as unobtrusively as possible. She focused on a metal tube sticking out of the water. It seemed to give off bursts of light, as if it were studded with prisms and mirrors reflecting the rays of the sun.

"Hey, see that thing over there? I wonder what it is!" she said, excited.

The others looked and George gasped. "It could be the periscope of a submarine!"

*The man shouted, "Get away from this island."*

"What!" Danny exclaimed. For a moment he forgot to keep his engine racing.

Nancy took the binoculars from Bess and trained them on the strange object. "Is the water deep enough for a submarine to get in?"

"Yes," Danny replied. "Notice that the thing is sticking out of one of the channels where the water is green. That means it's deep enough for a small sub. As a matter of fact, during World War II enemy subs got in here this way. The government had mined all the larger, more important channels to keep them out, but small enemy craft slipped in anyway."

"Danny, can you go into the channel?" Nancy asked. "I'd like to see if that really is a periscope."

"Sure," Danny said and changed course.

But they soon realized that the men on *The Whisper* had no intention of letting them go through with their plan.

"They're coming closer," George said tensely. "Obviously they don't want us to check that thing out there."

"Which proves that they have something to do with it," Bess added.

Again the other boat pulled alongside the *Pirate*. "You kids think I'm fooling!" the skipper shouted. "I'm not. If you don't turn around instantly, your boat is gonna get rammed. And it'll cost you a pretty penny to have it repaired!"

"But we're leaving the island," Danny pointed out. "Just as you told us to!"

"You're going in the wrong direction. Turn back!"

Danny hesitated. He realized that this time their pursuers meant business. Before he had a chance to pull the wheel around, *The Whisper* came so close to their skiff that it scraped the bow.

"All right! All right!" Danny cried out. "We're leaving. You don't have to damage us."

The skipper chuckled evilly. "And don't ever come back. You hear!"

Bess had turned white and sat frozen in her chair, her hands clamped tightly around its edge. Nancy and George realized that the situation was critical and did not object to Danny's pulling away in the direction the men had indicated.

*The Whisper* followed them for a while, then turned off. Obviously the men were satisfied that they had chased the intruders away.

"Wow!" Bess said finally. "I don't want to see those people ever again!"

Nancy grinned. "I do. They're up to no good, and I'm planning to find out what it is."

As the *Pirate* headed toward Key Biscayne, George said, "I wonder who those guys are. Let's stop at the Coast Guard office and see in whose name *The Whisper* is registered."

"We don't have to do that," Danny said. "My

dad has a book containing all the information. Unless it's a brand-new entry, it should be in there."

"I wish we could be sure that we saw a periscope," Nancy said, still pondering their strange experience.

"How do periscopes work?" Bess asked.

"Oh, I know that because we just had it in school," Danny volunteered. "You see, the periscope is the eye of the underwater craft. A submarine builder by the name of Simon Lake invented the first good periscope, which was way ahead of the technology and science of his time. He bought a lot of lenses and began to experiment."

"Not too complicated!" George said.

"Maybe not, but one day he hit upon a lucky combination. He could look down the street and see people walking and wagons rolling through the harbor. He called it an omniscope. It offered enough magnification and clearness of optics even for night vision, so it was a big success."

"How long ago was that?" George asked.

"Nineteen hundred two," Danny told her. "Before that they just had makeshift equipment."

As soon as they arrived at the Cosgrove house, Danny went to get the boat registry. It was large and heavy. He put it on the dining-room table. The girls peered over his shoulder as he checked "W" for *Whisper*.

"Ah. Here it is," he said triumphantly. "It belongs to two men, Matt Carmen and Breck Tobin. They live in Bridgeport, Connecticut."

"Do you know who they are?" Nancy asked.

"No. Never heard of them. I wonder what they're doing down here. They're a long way from home."

"I'm sure they're in league with the men who run the Crocodile Ecology Company," Nancy said.

"Maybe they're supposed to guard the place," George spoke up. "They got rid of us in a hurry!"

"I hope they don't check up on who owns the *Pirate* and then come here and bother us!" Bess said, worried.

Danny insisted upon being cheerful about the whole affair. "We may be boxed in, but we're not going to let those guys get the better of us!" he vowed.

Nancy smiled. "That's the spirit! The question is, what are we going to do next?"

When Mr. Cosgrove returned home, the young people told him what had happened and asked his opinion on the case. He thought for a few moments, then said, "Frankly, I'm puzzled. We now have a list of suspicious people, but we still have no idea of what they're up to."

"Or how the periscope fits in," Nancy added.

Mr. Cosgrove smiled. "Are you sure you weren't looking at a marker for a buoy?"

"I don't think so," Nancy replied. "But the only way to find out for sure will be to go back and look again."

"Maybe we shouldn't use the *Pirate*," Danny said. "Our enemies are familiar with it. Whenever they see us they'll come after us."

"What do you have in mind?" his father asked.

"Perhaps we could ask our friends the Piarullis if we can use their cabin cruiser." He turned to the girls. "They dock right next to us, and if they're not using the *Sampson*, I'm sure they'll let us have it. It's enclosed, too, which would help. Those men couldn't identify us."

"That's a good idea," Mr. Cosgrove agreed. "I'll call them and ask."

He went to the telephone and returned a few minutes later. "Mr. Piarulli said you can have his boat tomorrow. Unfortunately, their son and his wife are taking it up north the following day."

Danny grinned. "One day is better than none!"

"True," George agreed. "But what do we do after that?"

"Play it by ear," Danny said with a grin. "We'll take things as they come. Let's leave early in the morning. The tide should be just right."

"Do you think it's necessary for all of us to go?" Bess asked. "Mrs. Cosgrove promised to show me how to make Lemon Nut Cake. I don't want to pass up the opportunity to enlarge my knowledge of recipes."

"If you'd rather cook than be a detective, you're welcome to stay home," George said.

Bess could not stand her cousin's condescending tone. "On second thought, I'll postpone my culinery education," she decided.

Bess was relieved, however, when the plans changed abruptly later that evening. The Cosgroves and their guests were seated in the living room, discussing the mystery. The visitors were trying to figure out the connection between the men on Crocodile Island and the two from Connecticut when the telephone rang.

Mr. Cosgrove answered, then said, "Nancy, there's a long-distance call for you!"

## CHAPTER VI

## *The Impostor*

THE caller was Mr. Drew.

"I've had a long conversation with Roger Gonzales," he told Nancy. "He's eager to see you and has asked that you meet him at twelve o'clock tomorrow at his golf club. Mr. Cosgrove will give you directions. You're to tell the man at the desk that you're Miss Boonton."

Nancy did not reply immediately.

"Is something wrong?" her father asked.

"I don't know. Dad, have you any idea where Mr. Gonzales called from?"

"No. His house, I suppose. Why?"

"Because I think his phone is being tapped."

"Why do you say that?"

"His enemies knew all about our arrival," Nancy said, and told her father about the kidnapping attempt.

"I don't like this!" he exclaimed. "The case is more dangerous than I expected."

"One thing is sure," Nancy said. "Our masquerade is known. When we visited Crocodile Island, someone took our pictures."

"Great!" her father murmured. "Perhaps you should come home."

"Oh, no!" Nancy cried out. "Please, Dad, we'll manage. We have Danny to help us, and even though the crooks know who we are and why we're here, we'll figure out something to outsmart them. Besides, I have to keep my date with Mr. Gonzales tomorrow, so I can warn him."

"True," her father agreed. "If the Crocodile Ecology people overheard my conversation with Roger today, they'll probably try to follow you and prevent you from reaching the club. Keep that in mind."

"I will," Nancy promised. "Don't worry. I'll think of something."

"All right. And good luck!"

When Nancy told the others about the new developments, they agreed that she should meet Mr. Gonzales the following day.

"I suggest," Mrs. Cosgrove said, "that when you leave here you go shopping. Then take a cab to the club from a store. This way you won't be followed."

"That's a good idea," Nancy agreed. The next

day Mr. Cosgrove drove her to a department store, where she made a few purchases, then went out a side door and took a taxi. When Nancy arrived at the club, she went to the desk and asked for Mr. Gonzales. "I'm Miss Boonton," she added.

The clerk looked at her searchingly. "There must be some mistake," he said slowly. "Miss Boonton is already here."

"What!" Nancy was stunned by the announcement. So that's how her enemies had double-crossed her!

She asked the man for a piece of paper and a pencil, and quickly scribbled a note to Mr. Gonzales. Nancy explained the situation and asked if he would come to the lobby. Then she handed the note to the clerk.

"Would you please send this to Mr. Gonzales," she requested.

The clerk summoned a boy and within a few minutes, Nancy saw a handsome, dark-haired man of about fifty, wearing a white suit, approach the desk. The clerk motioned to the girl.

"This is Mr. Gonzales," he said.

Nancy nodded, then asked her father's friend to move a little distance away so they would not be overheard.

"I'm Nancy Drew," she whispered. "The Miss Boonton you're entertaining is an impostor."

Nancy opened her purse and showed Mr. Gonzales her driver's license. He looked at it, then at her, in amazement.

"How do you do," he said in a low voice. "I'm dreadfully sorry about this. Do you know who the other girl is?"

"No," Nancy replied. "Let's go inside and find out."

Quickly the two went to the dining room, and Mr. Gonzales led the way toward a table at the window. Suddenly he stopped short. "She's gone!" he exclaimed. "The other Miss Boonton is gone!"

Nancy was not surprised to hear it. She deduced that when Mr. Gonzales had received the note and gone to the desk, the girl realized that her trick had been discovered and she decided to disappear at once!

"She had a good head start!" the girl detective thought.

Nancy suggested that they give an alarm to the man at the main desk so he could ask the clubhouse guard and various workers on the grounds and golf course to look for the impostor.

Mr. Gonzales went to the headwaiter's desk and picked up the phone. Nancy heard him tell the story to the man in charge of the club and ask that a search be made for a tall, slender young woman with a lot of blond hair.

"She was wearing a white skirt and blouse,

with a red-and-white sleeveless vest," he said.

The message was passed along at once. Nancy, impatient to find out where the girl had gone, told Mr. Gonzales she wanted to do a little hunting on her own account. He offered to go with her.

"Where do you want to look first?" he asked.

"How about inspecting all the cars parked on the grounds? She might be hiding in one."

Mr. Gonzales led the way to the far side of the dining room and out a sliding glass door. A caddy came by, and Mr. Gonzales asked him if he had seen the girl. The answer was no, and the search went on. They checked every car in the area. All they found inside them was a sleeping dog in one with an open window, and a large teddy bear in another.

"Of course there's a third possibility," Nancy said. "The phony Miss Boonton could have been brought to the club by a friend, who could have waited for her."

"True," Mr. Gonzales agreed.

As they turned back to the clubhouse, Nancy stopped a couple who were driving in. She asked if they had seen a girl dressed in white except for a red-and-white vest. "We don't know whether she was on foot or in a car."

"No, we didn't," the man replied.

"Thank you," Nancy said, disappointed.

Moments later a sports car came from the opposite direction. Mr. Gonzales asked the driver if he had noticed a girl on the road.

"A blond wearing a red-and-white vest?" the man asked.

"That's right," Nancy answered, excited. "Where did you see her?"

"I passed her about a mile down the road. She was riding in a brown car with a man."

The information was sufficient for Nancy to conclude that the fraudulent Miss Boonton had made a quick getaway. "No use in looking for her any more," she told Mr. Gonzales.

He nodded. "I owe you a lunch. You must be starved. Let's return to the dining room."

After they had ordered salads and iced tea, Nancy and her host talked about the mystery.

"I don't understand how this could have happened," he said, puzzled.

"I do," Nancy said. "Your phone must be tapped. Do you remember where you were when you called my father on various occasions?"

Mr. Gonzales frowned. "The first call I made from home. The second one too—no, wait a minute. I made that one from the club. Yesterday I phoned from home again."

Nancy nodded. "That proves my theory," she said and told him about all that had happened, including the kidnapping attempt.

The man turned pale. "This means that not

only am I in great danger, but you are, too!" he said. "I never would have asked you to come here if I had known!"

"Mr. Gonzales," Nancy said, "I think you have more to worry about than I do. I have two friends with me, and a boy is helping us. We'll be all right. But you would probably be better off if you left this club as little as possible while we're working on the case."

Mr. Gonzales nodded. "I see your point, and I'll do as you say."

Nancy changed the subject. "You told my father that you were suspicious of your business partners. Who are they, and exactly what worries you?"

"There are three partners in the Crocodile Ecology Company," Mr. Gonzales said. "Hal Gimler, George Sacco, and me. Recently, the two active partners were evasive when I asked them about certain matters. I had a feeling they were dodging my questions about what's going on. I found out they made trips to Mexico numerous times, and I know we have no dealings with that country. I had the feeling that they were trying to deceive me."

"That's when you called Dad the first time?" Nancy asked.

"Right. When they realized I suspected them, they asked me to sell my interest in the company to them; and at one point I felt that would be the best thing to do. That was when I called your father the second time and canceled your reservations."

"But then you changed your mind?"

"Yes, because it turned out that I was not getting any cooperation at all from my partners. I'm glad you're here, but I don't like the idea of exposing you to danger."

"We're used to that," Nancy said dryly. "Tell me, have you ever seen a submarine or a periscope near Crocodile Island?"

"No. Why do you ask?"

Nancy told him how she and her friends had spotted a periscope, which had disappeared before they could get a closer look.

Mr. Gonzales frowned. "The company could be shipping out crocodiles and not listing the sales. A submarine would be a splendid way of concealing the transaction." He went on to say that some older reptiles had disappeared, and when he had inquired about them, his partners had merely said they had escaped.

"I don't see how they could have, with the fencing there is all around the island," Nancy commented.

"That's true," her companion agreed.

"How much of all this did you tell the other Miss Boonton?" Nancy asked.

"I mentioned that I was suspicious of Hal Gimler and George Sacco because I couldn't get straight answers out of them. Then you arrived and she took off."

"You didn't mention the phone calls to my father?"

"Only the first one."

By this time Mr. Gonzales and Nancy had finished eating. They left the table and walked to the entrance. The clerk at the desk called a taxi for Nancy. While waiting for it to arrive, she told Mr. Gonzales how much she had enjoyed talking with him.

"Now I'll work harder to solve your mystery."

"You've made a very good start," he said, patting her on one shoulder. "From here on I'll make calls only from the club or a public phone booth."

Nancy rode off to the Cosgrove home. When she arrived, the couple was alone with Bess.

"George and Danny went out in the borrowed boat," Bess said. "I thought they'd be back by now."

"They may have hit low tide," Mr. Cosgrove said. "Nancy, tell us how your luncheon date was. Did you get to the club all right?"

"I did, only someone else got there before me," Nancy said, and gave full details about the impostor.

"Incredible!" Mrs. Cosgrove burst out. "Just think of the nerve of that young lady, pretending to be you!"

"I don't like the whole thing," Mr. Cosgrove added. "These people are obviously very clever and don't shy away from anything underhanded."

"We'll be careful," Nancy said.

When Danny and George had not returned two hours later, she began to worry.

"Did they have another encounter with *The Whisper?*" she wondered.

# CHAPTER VII

## Sea Detectives

MRS. Cosgrove realized that Nancy was concerned, and tried to cheer her up. "Look, Danny is a very reliable boatman," she said. "They could have become stuck during low tide. Instead of sitting here and waiting, why don't we all go to see a friend of mine? She has a little private zoo, which I'm sure you would enjoy."

"That sounds great," Nancy said. "But before we leave, do you mind if I phone the Coast Guard and ask if they've had a report of an accident?"

"Of course not," Mrs. Cosgrove said. "Go ahead."

Nancy learned that no trouble had been reported and felt better.

"I'll stay here and wait for George and Danny," Mr. Cosgrove said. "You enjoy yourselves."

Mrs. Cosgrove drove her guests along the waterfront until they came to a large estate. She pulled in, stopped at the front door, and rang the bell. To her disappointment she was told by the woman who answered that her friend, Mrs. Easton, was away for the day, and so was the animal trainer.

"I'd like to show my visitors from the North your zoo," Mrs. Cosgrove said. "Is it all right?"

"Yes, indeed," the woman replied. "Go ahead. You'll probably meet Eric, our gamekeeper. He'll show you around."

The man was not in sight. Mrs. Cosgrove, who had been to the estate many times, drove on. She told the girls a bit about the birds, turtles, and snakes that were in large covered cages.

"That flamingo is gorgeous!" Bess exclaimed, watching the long-legged creature with the pink feathers and dignified-looking head walk daintily across a fenced-in lawn. In the center was a pool.

Mrs. Cosgrove pointed out an enormous turtle and remarked, "They live to a very old age. I've heard of some that had dates carved on their backs showing they were a hundred and twenty-five years old!"

In another wire-mesh enclosure were a variety of snakes.

"I'm not going to look at them!" Bess declared. "They give me the creeps."

Mrs. Cosgrove laughed. "If you lived in Flor-

ida, you'd have to get used to snakes. We have all
kinds and sizes. Some are beautiful, and all are
very graceful."

"I'll take your word for it," Bess said and was
glad when Mrs. Cosgrove passed the snake pen
and stopped the car some distance away. She and
the girls got out and walked to a spot directly
on the bay. Here there was a large enclosure, part
of it extending into the bay.

"A pair of crocodiles," Mrs. Cosgrove said,
resting her elbows on the cement fencing.

As the onlookers watched, one of the reptiles
got up and walked into the water. At the same
time Nancy spotted a canoe being paddled under
the overhanging mangrove trees along the shore.
In it were three boys. Without warning, one
threw a large piece of coral rock at the reptile.
Fortunately it missed.

The move annoyed the crocodile, however. He
turned back to join his mate. The boys in the
canoe paddled off quickly.

"I'm glad they're gone," Nancy said. "I'd hate
to see the croc injured."

Mrs. Cosgrove explained that the creature's
hide was so thick that it was almost impossible
to hurt its back. "But if something hits a crocodile in the eyes, it's very painful."

Bess asked, "Do these crocs have names?"

Mrs. Cosgrove smiled. "Yes. They're Lord and
Lady Charming."

Nancy and Bess laughed, and Bess remarked, "They don't look very charming to me."

As if he had heard her, the larger of the two crocodiles emitted a low growl, followed by a hiss. He opened his jaws wide.

Bess retreated in a hurry. "W-what's the matter with him?"

Suddenly several small fish, sucked up through a pipe running into the enclosure from the salt water, were sprayed into the pen. The crocodile forgot it was angry. With lightning speed he ran down into the water and grabbed several fish with his great jaws, then closed them with a resounding crack.

At this moment the canoe with the three boys returned. This time each of them was armed with large pieces of coral rock. They pitched them over the wall of the enclosure directly at the big reptiles. One of the rocks hit Lord Charming on one eye. It was obviously painful, for he began swishing madly in a circle, growling and hissing.

"Get away from here!" Nancy yelled at the boys. "Don't do that again!" The youngsters, looking scared, quickly paddled out of sight.

The crocodile swished his great tail back and forth so rapidly in the water that it sprayed into the air, soaking the onlookers.

"Eric!" Mrs. Cosgrove called frantically. "Eric, come quickly!"

The gamekeeper, a tall man with a gray beard,

ran toward the enclosure and looked at Lord Charming. "What's the matter?" he asked.

"His eye," Mrs. Cosgrove answered.

"Poor old fellow!" Eric said. "He's in pain, all right. I hope he won't lose the sight of that eye. Let me get something to put on it."

He hurried off and returned with a tube of salve and a pole with a hook on the end of it. Fearlessly he jumped over the cement wall and talked soothingly to the crocodile. "Sorry, old boy," he said. "Come now, Lord Charming, let me help you."

Nancy and her friends watched in fascination as Eric flipped the reptile onto his back with the pole, and squirted some of the salve into his injured eye.

All this time Lady Charming had been watching from a distance. When her mate turned over onto his stomach, she hurried forward. Using the pole for support, Eric leaped high over the concrete fence.

The visitors clapped. "You're marvelous," Mrs. Cosgrove said.

Eric grinned. "It's all in a day's work. Tell me how Lord Charming got hurt."

Nancy reported that three mean boys had come by in a canoe and hit the crocodile.

Eric scowled. "I can't stand people, big or little, who take advantage of a defenseless animal!"

"Where's the trainer today?" Mrs. Cosgrove asked.

"It's his day off," Eric replied. "You must come back when he's here. I'm sure you girls would enjoy the various acts he puts on with the animals."

"We will," Mrs. Cosgrove promised, then the visitors turned to leave.

When they reached home, George and Danny were back. They explained their delay, saying they had been caught in the low tide.

"Did you pick up any new clues?" Nancy asked.

"I think so," George replied. "We went all the way to Crocodile Island. There was no periscope in sight. But *The Whisper* was tied up at the dock. We got near enough to overhear voices. Apparently someone was talking on a radio telephone."

"What did he say?" Nancy asked eagerly.

"Tonight at eight," George replied.

"What do you think it meant?" Bess asked.

George said she and Danny had figured out that either someone was coming to the island or that *The Whisper* was taking off for a rendezvous with another boat.

Nancy was excited by the report. "I think you're right," she said. "Let's go out there this evening and see what happens."

Danny said that the tide would be perfect for

the trip. He turned to Mrs. Cosgrove. "Okay with you, Mother?"

She smiled. "It sounds like a great adventure. Of course, you must be careful not to get caught. You've been warned to stay away from that place, so take it easy!"

She packed a picnic supper for the young people, and before six o'clock Danny and the girls set off.

They ate the food on the way, and arrived at Crocodile Island before sunset. *The Whisper* left sometime later, and Danny followed it.

Nancy remarked that she was glad they were in a covered boat. "This way our enemies won't suspect we're in it, even if they see us," she said.

Danny nodded. "And the *Sampson* is powerful enough so we won't lose them," he said.

*The Whisper* headed out into the green channel and traveled for miles and miles.

"It seems as if they're going around the world," Bess said after dusk had come on. "Do we have enough gas to follow them?"

"Our supply won't last forever," Danny said, "but we can follow for several miles and still have enough gas for the return trip."

More time passed, then suddenly the young people spotted the vague outline of a large freighter. It was too dark to see its name or country of origin.

"I wonder if *The Whisper* is going to rendezvous with that ship," Nancy said. She took the binoculars out of their case and scanned the area. "They're both running without lights. Danny, I think we'd better turn ours off, too."

Danny complied and said, "I wonder if *The Whisper* and the freighter are still in motion." He flicked on the *Sampson's* sonar and detected the sound of *The Whisper's* motor. "The freighter is standing still and *The Whisper* is idling alongside," he said.

"Can we go any closer without being detected?" George asked.

"I think so," he replied. "We'll advance slowly. I'll keep the engine as low as possible."

"It's getting very misty out here," George observed. "I hope we'll be able to see what's going on."

Danny chuckled. "At least they won't see *us!*"

He drew up to within a hundred yards of *The Whisper* and cut his motor again. The four young people strained their eyes and ears, eager to find out why the two craft had met. Suddenly a bright searchlight was turned on, revealing the deck of the freighter and illuminating the smaller boat alongside it.

Nancy and her friends were terrified that they might be seen. Would the beam penetrate the mist far enough so the *Sampson* could be spotted?

# CHAPTER VIII

## Indian Tricks

THE four watchers in the *Sampson* held their breath. Would they be kidnapped and taken aboard the freighter?

Although the brilliant searchlight showed up the *Sampson* clearly, the two men paid attention only to the freighter. The young people observed a large pine box being lowered from the freighter to *The Whisper.*

Bess gave a little low scream. "Let's go!" she urged. "Somebody's going to be buried at sea!"

The others disagreed. Nancy said, "If that box were a coffin, there would be no need for a secret transfer. The freighter could have lowered it into the sea."

"Then what is it carrying?" Bess asked.

Nancy said she wished she knew that and where *The Whisper* would take the box.

Suddenly the great searchlight was turned off.

Then the regular lights on the freighter beamed again and its engines began to roar. Within seconds the large craft started to move northward.

"Where do you suppose it's going?" Danny asked.

"My guess," Nancy replied, "is Bridgeport, Connecticut. Remember, that's where the owners of *The Whisper* are from."

"What do you think the freighter brought?" George asked.

Nancy shrugged. "Obviously something very secret. Maybe it'll be buried on one of the keys, like pirate treasure."

"I think the box contains something they need on Crocodile Island," George suggested.

"I doubt that they need corpses," Bess said dryly.

Danny laughed. "Let's follow *The Whisper*. I'm sure it'll go back to the island. Perhaps we can find out what's in the pine box."

The lights of *The Whisper* were still out, but they could hear its motor running. Danny listened carefully, then frowned. "It sounds as if they're going out to sea!" he declared.

"Can we follow it?" Nancy asked, excited.

"We don't have that much fuel. Also, with no lights its almost impossible. It's so dark now we'd either lose *The Whisper* or run into it!"

"I have an idea," George said. "Why don't we return to Crocodile Island and wait? Perhaps *The*

*Whisper* is only making a detour to throw off anyone who might follow it and will come back to the island later."

"Good suggestion," Nancy agreed. The young people turned around. After a while, Danny put the lights back on.

"I'm glad we're getting away from that coffin," Bess said. "I don't ever want to see it again."

George looked at her. "You're probably right. There was a slain gangster in it, and *The Whisper* is going to dump him overboard into deep water so nobody will know where he's buried!"

"You're disgusting," Bess exclaimed.

George defended herself. "You brought it up, not the rest of us."

Danny and Nancy were laughing. "George," the boy said, "you ought to write horror stories. You'd make a lot of money."

"No thanks," she replied. "I'll stick to real mysteries, like the secret of Crocodile Island."

When Danny saw the outline of the key, he shut down the engine and turned off his lights again. The young people settled down to wait for *The Whisper* to arrive, passing the time by telling Danny about various adventures they had had in the past. However, hours dragged by and nothing happened. Finally Danny suggested that they go home.

"My parents will be worried if we don't show

up soon," he said. "And I really don't think *The Whisper* is coming back here tonight."

Everyone agreed, and Bess suggested that they report the incident to the police the following morning. Nancy reminded her that the authorities would not investigate without proof of their accusation.

"Right now we don't know if a crime has been committed. We're just assuming that something illegal is going on and we're angry at the skipper of *The Whisper,* because he chased us away from Crocodile Island. But that's not enough for the police."

When the young people reached home, the Cosgroves were relieved. "We were worried about you," Danny's mother said. "What happened?"

The girls reported the strange events, then Mrs. Cosgrove said, "A man called here, asking for Anne Boonton. I didn't know whether it was Mr. Gonzales or not, so I told him he had the wrong number."

"Good idea," Nancy said. "How did he react?"

"He just hung up and didn't call again."

For nearly an hour, Nancy, her friends, and the Cosgroves discussed what might have been in the box and where *The Whisper* had taken it.

Finally Mrs. Cosgrove said, "If the people on Crocodile Island were shipping something out illegally, the box would have been hauled up to the freighter, not the other way around. It appears as if Gimler and Sacco were receiving something illegal. But then, why didn't *The Whisper* take it back to the island?"

"That's a good question," Nancy said and gave a frustrated sigh. "Anyway, I'd like to go back in the morning. Perhaps we can pick up a clue to the puzzle."

Danny offered to accompany her, but said they would have to wait until noon for the right tide.

Mrs. Cosgrove spoke up. "In the meantime, why don't you girls visit Mrs. Easton again? I spoke to her tonight and she invited you—said you can come any time tomorrow. Their Indian animal trainer will be there all day and will be glad to show you his tricks. He's a Seminole from the Miccosukee tribe and his name is Joe Hanze."

"That sounds great," Bess said. "I'd much rather go there than to Crocodile Island!"

The others laughed and the following morning Danny and the girls borrowed Mrs. Cosgrove's car and set out for the zoo.

When they arrived, Nancy rang the front doorbell. Mrs. Easton greeted them and talked for a while, then she said, "I'm sure you'll enjoy watching Joe with the animals. He's very entertaining and well informed. Just drive around to the back of the house. You'll see his cottage. Tell him I sent you."

The girls thanked the friendly woman and

went to the Indian's place. Joe Hanze was a pleas-
ant man who spoke English fluently. His bronzed
face was handsome and his body muscular and
lithe. Nancy guessed that he was about fifty years
old.

Joe said he would be happy to show off his
tricks. On the way to the turtle pen, he asked the
girls if they knew anything about the background
of the Seminoles.

"No," Nancy told him. "I'd love to hear some
of their history."

Joe said that the original Seminoles had come
from Canada. The reason why they trekked south
was not known.

"Maybe it was the weather," he surmised. "In
any case, some of them got as far as Florida and
intermarried with other Indians who were already here. My great-grandfather came from
Canada. He was a fine hunter and earned a good
living on the way by trapping wild animals and
selling their hides."

"Where do your people live?" Bess asked.

"Up in the Everglades. Life there is rather
primitive, so I decided to come here when I was
a young man and get some education. I liked it
so much that I stayed. Whenever I want to see my
folks, I just get in a car and drive to the Everglades."

The group had reached the wire enclosure
where the giant turtle lived, and Joe went inside.

The reptile poked its head out of the shell and looked at him.

The Indian pulled a little musical pipe from his pocket and played a tune. To the girls' surprise, the turtle began to dance. When Joe stopped the music, the amusing creature went up and down on its forefeet as if bowing.

"Wonderful!" Bess exclaimed.

The girls clapped and laughed, and Joe said he would have the flamingo put on an act next. When he spoke to the beautiful pink-legged bird, it went over to him and touched the Indian's lips.

"Thank you for my morning kiss," Joe said. "Now suppose you do your war dance."

The flamingo flapped its wings up and down furiously while running around the lawn. At one point the bird soared off and the girls were worried that it might not return. In a few moments it came back and strode about in a circle. Every few feet the bird jumped high into the air and landed neatly a few yards away. When the flamingo became tired of showing off, it walked back to Joe.

"That's great!" George exclaimed. "You must have a lot of patience to train these creatures."

The Indian said he loved animals and did not find it hard to work with any of them. "Now let's go over and call on Lord and Lady Charming," he added.

On the way Joe stopped at a large toolshed. He

opened the door and the girls noticed a refrigerator inside. Joe took out a large chunk of meat that he wrapped in paper. He rejoined the girls and said to Nancy, "I want you to feed this to Lord Charming when I tell you."

"Is this breakfast or lunch?" George asked, grinning.

Joe smiled. "It's just a snack. Watch how fast it disappears!"

When they arrived at the concrete wall that surrounded the crocodile pen, he picked up a pole from the edge, then jumped over the fence and walked up to the reptile who was resting on the sand.

"Lady Charming," he said, "you'd better flip over and not give us any trouble."

He prodded her with the spiked pole until he was able to flip her over. Now she would take a few minutes to get back on her feet.

Lord Charming was lying in the water at one end of the pen, under the shade of the mangrove trees that hid the wall of the pen at this point. As Joe approached him, he said to the girls, "Notice his eyeteeth and see how they protrude below the gums? That's one way you can tell the difference between an alligator and a crocodile. The alligator's teeth are more even and do not show below the jaw when it's tightly closed."

He went on to say that Nancy was to throw the meat after he got the crocodile to open his jaws. She figured that from the angle where she stood, her aim would be poor, so she vaulted the fence and stood at the edge of the water.

Joe looked worried. "I wanted you to throw it over the fence!" he said. "But maybe Lord Charming will behave if you don't make a fuss."

He tossed a little stone, which hit the crocodile lightly on the snout. At once his jaws opened. Instantly Nancy threw the chunk of beef. Her aim was perfect and the meat disappeared within a second.

Nancy was so fascinated as she watched the reptile that she failed to retreat. Suddenly the crocodile moved its great tail. In a moment it would hit Nancy hard and injure her!

"Look out!" George shouted.

## CHAPTER IX

## *Hurricane Legend*

WITH a leap Nancy cleared the top of the concrete wall surrounding the crocodile pen. She avoided the swishing tail by inches!

Joe shouted at the reptile in the Seminole language and prodded him with his heavy wooden pole. Finally the creature became quiet and the Indian hurried out of the pen.

Nancy jumped to the ground, still trembling slightly. She looked over the wall and said, "Lord Charming, your manners are pretty bad. That was no way to thank me for the meat."

Joe grinned. "Crocodiles aren't house pets, you know. I'm glad nothing happened."

Bess spoke up. "You almost gave me a heart attack, Nancy. I'm sure I would have been too terrified to jump over that wall."

George chuckled. "I'll bet you would have.

But then, I doubt that you'd have gone into the pit in the first place."

Joe stood shaking his head. "You're some girl," he said to Nancy.

She smiled, then changed the subject. "Just before I threw that chunk of meat, I saw a man peering at me from among the trees. He didn't look one bit friendly."

"That's strange," Joe said. "The only other person who works here is Eric, and he's not around this morning."

"It wasn't Eric," Nancy said. "We met him the other day."

"What did this guy look like?" George asked.

"He had long black hair, small eyes, and looked like an Indian," Nancy whispered, not wishing to hurt Joe's feelings.

"I'll search for him," Danny offered and ran in the direction Nancy had indicated.

Joe joined in the hunt, but both of them returned a little while later without having seen the stranger.

"I noticed footprints along the shore," Danny reported. "They led toward the water. Whoever the man was, he wore a small-sized shoe with a rippled sole. When I reached the spot where the prints stopped, I saw a man in a small motorboat too far away to recognize. If he was the fellow who was watching us, Nancy, he's gone."

Joe promised to look out for the stranger in case he should return, then the young people thanked him for the tour of the zoo and went home. After a quick lunch, they set out in the skiff for Crocodile Island.

"Do you think that man was spying on us this morning?" Bess asked while they were gliding along in the water.

"Maybe he was a sneak thief who was trying to make off with something from the estate," Danny suggested. "When he saw us, he ran."

"It's possible," Nancy agreed. "But it's more likely that Bess is right. He could have followed us from your house to see what we were doing."

George looked behind them. "No one is following us now. Let's stop worrying about him."

The young people once again passed the stilts with cottages built on top of them, and it occurred to Nancy that they might pick up a clue to Crocodile Island from one of the inhabitants.

"After all, they live close to the place," she said. "Danny, do you think we might stop and call on the owners?"

"Why not?" he replied, and paused at each cottage. He received no answer to his "Hello? Anybody home?" Finally he laughed. "There aren't any boats tied up at the posts. Obviously no one is here."

As they passed a group of posts with nothing

on them, Bess shivered. "Every time I think about a cottage being blown away in a hurricane, I worry about whether people were in it or not."

"I never heard of any," Danny said. "But did you know that crocodiles were blown here by hurricanes?"

The girls laughed and George said, "Don't kid us!"

"I'm not kidding," Danny replied. "The story comes from the Indians. They say that when the Seminoles arrived here many, many years ago, there were plenty of alligators, but no crocodiles. Then, after a terrific hurricane, crocodiles were seen along the shore of Key Biscayne."

Nancy, curious, asked, "Where did the crocodiles come from?

"Supposedly from Cuba," Danny answered. "But they might even have traveled all the way from Africa."

"Oh, yes?" George said. "If I see that in a science book I'll believe it, but not from hearsay."

"Well, they got here somehow," Danny defended himself. "And certainly no one brought them. You figure it out."

He sent his boat past the houses on stilts. The *Pirate* had not gone far when he pointed out an uninhabited key. "That's a good picnic spot," he said. "Friends of mine and I sometimes come here."

George asked if he could go closer. "I see a green bottle floating toward shore. Let's pick it up!"

Bess saw a good chance to tease her cousin. She rarely got the opportunity. "Are you collecting old bottles?" she asked. "From here that doesn't look very valuable."

"Possibly not," George retorted, "but it's corked. Maybe there's something valuable inside."

When Danny reached the spot, George got down from her chair, leaned over the gunwale, and grabbed the bottle out of the water. It was dark green and had no markings. She tried to uncork it, but at first the stopper would not budge.

"I guess we'll have to take the bottle home and work on it with a corkscrew," Bess said.

"Maybe not," George replied. She wiggled the cork from left to right, being careful not to break it. The cork loosened little by little. With one final yank, George pulled it out.

She turned the bottle upside down. Nothing fell out. Then she held it up to her nose.

"What does it smell like?" Bess asked. "Perfume?"

"Nothing," George said, disappointed.

"You might as well throw it back into the water," Danny advised.

"I guess you're right," George said. "The whole thing was—wait a minute!" She had given the bottle a hard shake and looked into it. "I see something inside!" she said, excited. "It might be a note!"

Everyone watched breathlessly as George held the bottle upside down and continued to shake it. Finally a rolled paper appeared in the long, thin neck. She reached in with one finger and gently eased the piece out.

"What is it?" Nancy asked.

George carefully unrolled the yellowed, crinkled paper. "It's a message!" she cried out. "Dated twenty years ago!"

"What does it say?" Danny asked impatiently.

"*Captain Wayne,*" George read, "*USS Venerable sank in hurricane off Argentina. Twelve took to life boat. God's blessings.*"

There was complete silence for several seconds, then Nancy asked to see the paper.

"I believe it's authentic," she said after examining it carefully. "The paper is well preserved and the cork was in tight. And down in the corner is a date. This was written twenty years ago!"

"Why don't we take the whole thing to the Naval Station at Key West?" Danny suggested. "They have all kinds of records there of old ships that went down in hurricanes."

"Good idea," George said. She was about to

*"It's a message!"* George cried.

roll the note and put it back in the bottle, when Bess stopped her.

"Don't do that," her cousin advised. "It was hard enough to get it out the first time. Shoving it back in the bottle won't make it any more authentic, you know."

George laughed and slipped the message in her pocket, then replaced the cork in the bottle. "My dear cousin, you're right for a change."

"I'm right more often than you want to admit," Bess said haughtily.

Danny grinned and started the *Pirate's* engine. Soon they approached Crocodile Island. The girls used the binoculars to search for the periscope in the deep, green channel, but did not see it. They circled the island from a distance and noticed a sign at the landing platform: NO VISITORS TODAY.

"They're keeping everyone out," Danny said. "No activity at all. I wonder for how long."

Nancy shrugged. "Let's just keep going around the island. Maybe we'll see something sooner or later."

They had almost completed the second circle when they heard an agonizing cry from somewhere on the island!

# CHAPTER X

## *The Runaway's Clues*

BESS turned pale. "Wh-what was that?"

Before anyone could guess, there were more bloodcurdling screams from the island.

"Maybe a crocodile got one of the workers!" George cried out in alarm.

Just then a young bearded man raced from behind the mangrove trees into the water. He splashed through the shallow area, and when he reached the green channel began to swim.

Seeing the nearby boat, he cried out, "Save me! Save me!"

Danny guided the skiff alongside the frantic swimmer, and the girls pulled him aboard. His eyes were bulging with terror, and his legs were bleeding profusely.

Danny quickly got a first-aid kit from a locker and handed it to the girls. They carefully washed the stranger's wounds and applied a soothing salve.

"What happened to you?" Nancy asked him.

"Just—just don't take me back to the island, please!" the young man pleaded.

"Of course not. Did a crocodile bite you?"

"No, no! I was beaten with one of the sharp hooked poles they use on the reptiles."

"How dreadful!" Bess said. "Why would anyone do that to you?"

"Because I didn't clean the pits to suit the boss. Oh, he has a terrible temper!"

Nancy wound a bandage around the man's left leg, while George attended to the right one.

Danny looked back to see if they were being followed, then asked, "Where do you want to go?"

"To Key Biscayne," the fugitive replied.

The young people heard the sound of an engine and noticed a fast motorboat coming up in the deep channel toward the island.

Just then a man appeared at the shore, yelling at the top of his lungs. "Colombo! Colombo, where are you? You can't run away! Where are you, Colombo?"

The runaway lay down in the bottom of the skiff, well protected by the three girls. He trembled with fright.

Danny put on extra power, and the *Pirate* skipped speedily across the bay. The man on shore continued to yell for Colombo, but suddenly he addressed the skipper of a passing motorboat.

"Follow the *Pirate!*" he ordered, pointing.

"The water's not deep enough," the skipper replied, much to the relief of Danny and his passengers.

The fugitive sighed, and Nancy asked him who he was and what had happened on Crocodile Island.

"My name is Colombo Banks. I'm from New Orleans, but I came here to get a job. I was hired to work on Crocodile Island. At first I liked it, but then the bosses became very cruel."

"In what way?" Nancy asked.

Colombo said that although he had requested permission to make a trip into Biscayne Bay on his free days, he had always been refused.

"I began to wonder why, and finally decided that the members of the Crocodile Ecology Company were doing something underhanded. Perhaps they didn't want me to leave and tell people what I had seen or heard."

"What did you see and hear?" George spoke up.

Colombo told them that a speedboat called *The Whisper* came and went mysteriously.

"Mysteriously? How?" Nancy asked.

"Often it docks or leaves in the middle of the night, and I was never allowed to watch what was going on. The bosses made me sleep on the

far side of the island with one other man named
Sol. He's black and a great guy. We were friends,
but four other fellows who work there stay in the
main house with the bosses."

"How mean!" Bess exclaimed.

Colombo went on, "I decided to find out what
was going on. At night I would sneak out of my
cabin and go to the main part of the island. Many
times I saw Mr. Sacco and Mr. Gimler at the landing dock, but usually they whispered and I
couldn't overhear anything.

"Once, however, Gimler spoke loud enough
to a man I'd never seen. 'They want five hundred,' the boss said. 'Can you carry that many?'
Unfortunately I couldn't make out the answer."

"Whom was he talking to?" George inquired.

"The skipper of *The Whisper*."

"Do you think they were referring to crocodiles?" Danny asked.

"I don't know."

"Do they ever transport crocs in *The Whisper?*"

"No," Colombo replied, then added, "I was
scolded a good deal, mostly for no reason. It
seemed as if the bosses had a grudge against me.
I think they figured I knew more than I really do."

"That's possible," Nancy said thoughtfully.

"I wanted to leave the job," Colombo went on,
"but they would never let me. A few times I tried
to sneak up to the visitors and ask for a ride. But

one of the workmen who lived with the bosses always chased me away."

"Did Sacco and Gimler ever have anything delivered to the island, or did they do the shopping themselves?" Nancy asked.

Colombo said that as far as he knew all supplies were brought in by *The Whisper,* and whenever any of the men left, they used that boat.

"You mean," Nancy asked, "that they do not use any other means of transportation?"

"Not as far as I know. But then, I wasn't around to see everything. I just worked and ate and slept."

The young people felt sorry for the man, and his story made them more suspicious than ever of the partners in the Crocodile Ecology Company. By now they had reached Key Biscayne. Danny pulled into a public dock to let Colombo off, and asked him if they could be of any further help.

Colombo shook his head. "You've all been mighty kind, and I'll never forget it. If I can ever do you a favor, just let me know."

Nancy asked him where he would stay.

"At the YMCA," he said. "I have relatives here, but Mr. Gimler knows about them. If I go there, he'll track me down and try to force me to return to Crocodile Island by threats, and make up some story."

"That's true," Nancy said. "Well, I hope your

legs will heal properly. Perhaps you should see a doctor."

Colombo smiled. "I think you ladies did a fine job. I'll be well in no time." He stepped onto the dock with Danny's help, then turned around. "I don't even know your names," he said.

Nancy hesitated, but Danny spoke up quickly. "I'm Danny Cosgrove, and these are the Boonton girls, Anne, Elizabeth, and Jackie."

"Thank you," Colombo said. "I really appreciate your help."

Danny pushed off. "I hope you girls don't mind what I told him," he said. "But he can find out from anyone around here who owns the *Pirate*."

"That was perfectly all right," Nancy said. "Besides, I think we can trust him."

On the way home the young people discussed what the phrase "they want five hundred" could have meant.

"If not crocodiles, what else?" George asked.

"The thing that bothers me most," Bess said, "is that Mr. Gimler might have known Colombo was on the skiff. If so, he may make trouble. We'd better not go back to Crocodile Island."

"We've got to, Bess," said Nancy. "We're just beginning to get some good clues!"

When they reached the Cosgrove home, Danny's mother was waiting for them. After greeting each one, she said, "I have a message for you, Nancy."

"Yes? What is it?"

"Mr. Gonzales called. He has some valuable information to give you."

"Did he give any hint as to what it was?" Nancy asked.

Mrs. Cosgrove shook her head. "He said that you would receive a letter in the morning."

Nancy wanted to phone Mr. Gonzales at once, but realized that she should not let her curiosity get the better of her and possibly embarrass him.

Later in the evening, the group settled down to watch television, but the young detective had trouble concentrating on the show. Instead, her thoughts focused on what Colombo had told them about Crocodile Island.

Presently the phone rang. Mrs. Cosgrove answered, then handed the receiver to Nancy. "It's for you."

"Hello?" Nancy said.

"You're not Anne Boonton!" a man said gruffly. "You're Nancy Drew. We know all about you. If you and your friends don't leave Florida at once, you'll *never* get home again!"

# CHAPTER XI

## An Identification

"Who are you?" Nancy asked the man on the phone.

There was no reply, only a click in her ear.

Nancy's friends looked at her questioningly. "Who was it?" George asked.

"One of our enemies, I'm afraid. He told us to leave Florida, or we might never see our homes again!"

"Oh, dear!" Bess wailed. "Now they know where we're staying."

"So what?" George said. "This isn't the first time Nancy has been threatened over the phone by her adversaries!"

Danny tried to break the tension. "Bess, will you stop worrying? After all, you have me to protect you!"

Bess laughed, and after a while the mysterious call was forgotten.

Next morning Nancy watched eagerly for the mailman. When he came up the street, she ran from the house to meet him. He smiled at her and asked, "Is a Miss Anne Boonton staying here?"

"Yes," Nancy replied. "Do you have a letter for her?"

"Indeed I do," the man replied. "And a lot of others. You want to take them?"

"I'll be glad to," Nancy said, and he handed her the bundle.

She thanked him, then hurried into the house and quickly scanned the stack. The one addressed to Anne Boonton was near the bottom. Nancy opened the envelope. The letter read:

> Dear Anne:
>
> I had a phone call from Hal Gimler today. He told me that one of our employees, Colombo Banks, has run away. He suspects that the workman escaped in a skiff with three girls and a boy in it.
>
> Gimler thinks that Colombo may cause trouble and asked me to locate him. I was wondering, was your group responsible for his rescue, and do you know where he is? Gimler threatens to have him arrested for stealing.
>
> If you have any information about Colombo, meet me at my club for lunch tomorrow.
>
> G.

"That's today," Nancy said to herself.

By this time Bess, George, and the Cosgroves had joined her and wanted to know what the letter said. She read it to them.

When she finished, Mr. Cosgrove said, "You'd better go to the club and talk to Mr. Gonzales."

"There's only one problem," George said. "Nancy might be followed. Now that the Ecology people know where we're staying, they may have this place staked out."

"Well," Mr. Cosgrove said, "we belong to the same club as Mr. Gonzales, and we know many other members. Perhaps you could meet one of them and get a ride."

"That's a good plan," Nancy said. "Now we just have to figure out how I get from here to wherever I'll meet this person."

Bess had a suggestion. "Danny and Nancy are about the same size. Couldn't she wear his clothes and cover her hair with a golf hat?"

Nancy laughed. "I wouldn't want to have lunch with Mr. Gonzales in dungarees and a T-shirt!"

"True," Mrs. Cosgrove agreed. Then her face lit up. "I have it!" she said. "The delivery boy from Drummond's Market is due here at about eleven. He drives a van. I'll tell him to back up to our attached garage so you can slip into the van unseen. Then he can drop you off downtown."

"That sounds great," Nancy agreed.

"Okay. I'll call my friend Mrs. Grote and see

if she's playing golf today. If so, she can meet you at a drugstore on the main street. She has to pass it on the way to the club. What shall I tell her you'll be wearing?"

"If I put on my dark-blue pants suit, I might still be taken for a boy from a distance, provided I cover my hair," Nancy replied.

Mr. Cosgrove said he had a hat he used on the golf course, and offered to lend it to Nancy. "Come with me and see if it fits," he said.

While Nancy was gone, Mrs. Cosgrove called her friend, who agreed to pick up Nancy at the drugstore.

Ten minutes later the girl detective appeared again, dressed in a blue pants suit with white collar and cuffs, and the white golf hat.

"Oh, you look cute!" Bess exclaimed. "Not quite like Danny, but close!"

Just then Danny walked into the room and overheard Bess's remark. "You've got to be kidding!" he protested. "I don't own a fancy getup like that, and if I did, I'd give it away quick!"

Everyone laughed, and Nancy said, "All that counts is that from a distance I don't look like me!"

"Nancy," Mrs. Cosgrove said, "Mrs. Grote will meet you at the drugstore. She'll be wearing a white dress with a multicolored embroidered belt."

Soon the delivery boy arrived at the back door

in a van. Mrs. Cosgrove gave him the necessary in-
structions, and Nancy slipped into the rear. After
he had left the street she climbed into the seat
next to him. He looked at her and gave a low
whistle. "You're a doll" he said appreciatively.
"Are you on a secret date?"

Nancy smiled. "Suppose you guess?"

"I'm sure you are," the young man said as he
pulled around a corner, "so I won't interfere.
But I'd like to take you out myself some time."

"That's very kind of you," Nancy replied.
"Right now, however, I have to go on an important errand."

When they reached the drugstore, she thanked
the boy, quickly hopped out, and went inside.
She saw a rack of books and walked over to ex-
amine the titles. Just then an attractive woman
walked into the store. She was dressed in white
except for an embroidered, many-colored belt.

"She must be Mrs. Grote," Nancy concluded.
The woman spotted her at the same moment, and
walked toward the girl, holding out her hand.
"Anne, I'm Mrs. Grote. I'll be very happy to
drive you to the club."

They left the store by the rear entrance, where
Mrs. Grote had parked her car. Nancy was relieved. If anyone had followed the van and was
waiting for her in front, he would be fooled!

"Are you enjoying your visit here?" Mrs. Grote
asked as she drove off.

"Oh, yes," Nancy replied. "It has been very exciting."

"In what way?" Mrs. Grote asked.

Nancy did not want to give any details concerning the mystery, so she merely talked about their interesting boat rides, their trip to the Easton estate, and the show the Indian had put on.

Soon Mrs. Grote drove into the club grounds, so it was not necessary for Nancy to explain any further. She thanked the woman for picking her up and wished her a good score in her golf game.

Mr. Gonzales was seated in the lobby. "I'm so glad you came," he said, and led her to the dining room.

While they were eating, Nancy told him about Colombo and what he had said regarding the officers of the Crocodile Ecology Company.

"I'm not surprised," Mr. Gonzales commented.

Nancy mentioned the phrase: *They want five hundred. Can you carry that many?* "Mr. Gonzales, have you any idea what that could have meant?"

The man furrowed his brow. "No, I haven't. Surely they couldn't have been talking about crocodiles. There wouldn't be enough to fill such a big order."

"Do you raise anything else on the island that they could have referred to?" Nancy asked.

"No, nothing. I could ask my partners, but if I do they will know that I received word from

Colombo. Then they are likely to go after the poor man and harm him."

"You're right," Nancy agreed. "Would you like to speak to Colombo personally?"

"Indeed I would. Do you know how to reach him?"

"I'll try. Colombo said he would be staying at the YMCA."

Nancy stood up and went to a phone booth in the lobby. Luckily the receptionist at the Y confirmed that Mr. Banks was registered and offered to get him. Soon he was on the line.

"Hello?" he said hurriedly. His voice sounded frightened.

"Hello, Colombo," Nancy replied. "It's Anne Boonton. Could you meet me at this club?" She gave the address. "A friend of mine wants to speak to you about Crocodile Island. Take a taxi. I'll pay for it."

"All right," he said. "I'm glad it's you and not one of my former bosses. I'll be there as soon as I can."

Half an hour later the man arrived. Nancy hurried outside to pay the cabbie, then took Colombo to the tropical garden to meet Mr. Gonzales. When the young man heard that he was one of the partners in the Crocodile Ecology Company, he looked at Nancy apprehensively.

"Don't worry," she said. "Mr. Gonzales is not

like the other men. He wants to find out what's going on at Crocodile Island and if his partners are dishonest."

This reassured Colombo and he talked freely about the hardship he had suffered and the things he had observed.

"I'm in real trouble," he finished. "I've been trying to find a job but haven't been successful. I'm running out of money, but I'm afraid to contact my relatives for fear of being tracked down by Gimler."

"Perhaps I can help," Mr. Gonzales offered. "I heard the other day that one of the men in the club kitchen is quitting. Wait here, and I'll see what I can find out."

He went to the lobby to talk to the manager, and returned a few minutes later with a smile on his face.

"You're in luck, Colombo," he said. "Do you know how to prepare seafood?"

Colombo grinned. "I did that in New Orleans. But I never cut up a crocodile!"

Nancy laughed, and Mr. Gonzales asked Colombo to come along with him to see the head chef in the kitchen.

"We won't be long," he told Nancy.

Within ten minutes the two were back with a third man, who proved to be the pastry chef. Mr. Gonzales said that this man had finished his work and was about to drive home. He would take Colombo with him.

The cook went to get his car. Meanwhile, Nancy was told that Colombo had been given the job and was to report for work the next morning.

Colombo said, "I certainly appreciate what you've done for me."

Mr. Gonzales patted him on the back. "We're glad to help, and thank you for some good clues. If you think of anything else about the Crocodile Ecology Company, leave a note for me at the desk."

"I will," Colombo promised, then hurried outside, where the pastry chef was waiting for him.

When Nancy returned to the Cosgroves' home, no one was there. She knew where a key was hidden and went to get it. As she entered the hall, Nancy saw a note from George lying on the table. It said that Danny and the girls had gone to the small local Naval Station with the bottle George had found in the water. "Maybe we can find out about it without going to Key West," George had written.

At this moment, George was telling her story to a friendly young captain named Smith. He agreed that the old note appeared to be authentic and said he would try to verify its contents.

He stood up and went to a shelf containing books and registries. George meanwhile walked around his small office and glanced at photographs on the wall. Suddenly she stopped in front of a group picture of sailors. One of the faces looked familiar!

"Bess," George said, excited, "come here a moment. Doesn't this man remind you of someone?"

"Matt Carmen or Breck Tobin!" Bess answered. "Only the sailor's a lot younger."

As Captain Smith turned around, George asked who the sailor was.

# CHAPTER XII

## *Child in Danger*

CAPTAIN Smith turned over the picture George had pointed out. He read the names on the back and said, "This fellow is Giuseppe Matthews. I'll look up his record."

After a search in several volumes, he came across the item. "Matthews went AWOL," Captain Smith explained, "and was never heard from again. Why did you ask about him?"

George replied, "We've met a man who looks very much like the one in this picture. He's older, but there's a strong resemblance."

"Where did you see him?" Captain Smith asked.

"Out in the bay, near Crocodile Island. If he's the same person, he's using a different name now."

"What is it?" Smith inquired.

"Matt Carmen or Breck Tobin," George answered. "We were never introduced so we don't know which name goes with whom."

"You realize, of course, that we're still looking for Matthews," Captain Smith said. "And that we'll have to arrest him when we find him. Can you tell me where these men live?"

For a moment George hesitated. "What if one of them is the wrong person?" she asked. "I wouldn't want to get anyone in trouble."

"If they're not Giuseppe Matthews, they won't get into trouble," the captain pointed out.

"We saw a boat called *The Whisper*," Danny said. "We checked in a registry of ships and learned that it belongs to two men from Bridgeport, Connecticut. One of them is Matt Carmen, the other Breck Tobin."

Captain Smith wrote the information on a pad, and said he would follow up the lead. Then he checked another set of records for proof that the note in the bottle was authentic. Finally he smiled.

"Here it is," he said. "This is really amazing. A ship named *Venerable* was last heard from in Argentina. Her captain was George Wayne. This is the first message received since then."

"No one reported that she was wrecked?" Bess asked.

"No. And this note must have traveled at least ten thousand miles. I presume it would be considered part of the *Venerable's* records, so I'd like to keep it if you don't mind."

"Of course not," George said.

"Perhaps we can locate relatives of the captain and the crew, who would like to see it," Captain Smith added. He thanked the girls for bringing him their find and remarked, "The government may give you a citation for this."

George grinned. "That would be fun. I've never had one."

The girls said good-by to the captain and returned home. There was plenty of exciting conversation as they exchanged stories with Nancy. Mr. and Mrs. Cosgrove listened and were thunderstruck at all that had been learned.

"Each day you prove more and more what good detectives you are," their host complimented them.

"But we haven't solved anything yet," Nancy reminded him. She turned to George. "Did you ask Captain Smith about the periscope?"

"Oh dear, I didn't even think of that," George said. "But we can go back another time and inquire if he's ever heard of a sub around here."

Nancy wanted to go out in the skiff the following day, but Mr. Cosgrove said that he had had the craft out in the morning and found that it had been tampered with.

"It was lucky I discovered the damage before you used the *Pirate* again. You might have had a bad accident."

Nancy exclaimed, "You say it has been sabotaged? I'm afraid our enemies have been at work!"

The others agreed. Mrs. Cosgrove was worried. "This could mean that we're all being watched by spies. I think you should stay away from Crocodile Island for a while."

George grimaced. "At least until the *Pirate* is repaired."

"Meanwhile, why don't you visit Cape Florida?" their hostess suggested. "It's a lovely place. Beautiful trees and a nice beach. People go there for picnics. The main attraction is an old lighthouse. A guide will show you around and tell you something about its history."

"That sounds great," Bess said. "I could use a change of pace."

The girls got directions and set off early the next morning in one of the Cosgrove cars. Nancy, at the wheel, drove across the bridge leading to Cape Florida, and turned into the park entrance.

"Look at those gorgeous trees!" Bess exclaimed as they rode down an avenue of tall Australian pines.

"I've read in a magazine that these aren't native to Florida," Nancy said. "They were imported."

The road twisted and turned; then they came to a shaded picnic area with a large sandy beach.

"This is a heavenly spot," Bess remarked. "No wonder it's so popular."

Many people were seated on the beach, while

others had settled at picnic tables set up in a grove of trees. Nancy parked and the girls strolled toward the water.

To their right was a natural coral breakwater, which had been built up by polyps. It was very rough and Nancy realized at once that anyone slammed into it by waves could be badly cut. She noticed that bathers seemed to be avoiding it.

"What a lot of seaweed there is!" George remarked.

She picked up handfuls of it and rolled the soggy masses into a ball. "Let's play catch," she suggested.

The girls formed a triangle and threw the seaweed ball back and forth to one another. Whoever dropped it was eliminated from the game. After about ten minutes of play George was declared the winner.

To tease her, Bess picked up the ball and threw it hard at her cousin. Unfortunately it missed and sailed across the sand. The soggy mass landed *plunk!* on a bald-headed bather who was stretched out on the beach, sleeping.

"Oh!" Bess cried in dismay and went over to the man.

He blinked at her and looked annoyed, but after she apologized and he saw the look of concern on her face, he sat up and smiled. "Hi!" he said. "My, you're pretty!"

Bess backed away. "He's old and fat and bald-headed," she told herself. "I hope he won't try to get too friendly!"

Her fears were confirmed when the man stood up and took her hand. "I believe you threw that seaweed on purpose to wake me up. Well, here I am, at your service!"

"I—I—it was an accident," Bess stammered. Then she turned away and ran off as fast as she could. When she reached Nancy and George, they laughed.

"That'll teach you to aim straight when you throw something," George remarked.

Nancy, who had been watching various bathers in the water, now spotted a little girl who had not noticed that the tide was pulling her toward the coral breakwater. She realized that at any moment the child would be bashed against its jagged side and severely injured!

Nancy rushed down to the water's edge, slipped off her sandals, and splashed in. The water was shallow for adults, but the little girl could have drowned in it. Nancy swam with powerful crawl strokes toward her. By now the child was only a few feet from the breakwater!

"Come here!" Nancy called out and grabbed the child's hand. Together they struggled to the beach, where they were met by a frantic woman.

"Tessie!" she scolded. "You were told not to wade over there!"

The little girl cried. "I didn't mean to, but all

of a sudden I couldn't keep from going that way,"
she sobbed.

"Are you her mother?" Nancy inquired.

"No. I'm Mrs. Turnbull. I'm in charge of a
group of children who attend my day camp. I
brought them here to swim, but it's hard to watch
all of them at once."

"I understand," Nancy said.

"Thank you for going in after Tessie," Mrs.
Turnbull continued. "When I saw her, it was too
late for me to help."

Now the other children ran to them. The
woman opened her purse and offered Nancy a
bill as a reward for saving Tessie's life.

"Thank you," Nancy said, "but I couldn't possibly accept any money."

Tessie had stopped crying. She took Mrs.
Turnbull by the hand, and said, "I know how we
can reward her. Give her the map."

Mrs. Turnbull smiled. "Tessie, we have no
right to give the map away. We should turn it
over to the authorities. But I will show it to this
young lady. By the way, what is your name?"

Nancy introduced herself and her friends, who
had joined the group, by their Boonton name, not
wishing to be identified. The woman fished in her
handbag and brought out a faded piece of paper.
She unfolded it.

"I don't know whether this is authentic or not,"
she said. "We found it back in the woods. Somebody must have dropped it yesterday or today."

Nancy, Bess, and George studied the map. Not only was the paper old, but the printing on it was quite faded. Mrs. Turnbull explained that she and the children suspected that someone had been hunting for a treasure, perhaps buried long ago by pirates.

"The person must have lost it. The map does seem to indicate a buried treasure," she said. "Perhaps it's here on Florida Key."

The girls were intrigued by the story, and Nancy looked closely at the map. On it were directional lines pointing north, east, south, and west. There were also a number of intersecting lines converging at one spot.

"This must be the place where the treasure was hidden," Nancy remarked.

"True," Mrs. Turnbull said. "But how would one go about trying to figure out where it is?"

"We have to find a point of reference," Nancy said. "But what?" She puckered her brows and tried to figure out the strange map. Suddenly the girl detective had an idea.

"You see this line running directly into the water? It could be the coral breakwater!"

"You're right!" Mrs. Turnbull agreed. "Let's draw a continuing line from it through the sand and then bisect it just as it was on the map."

Tessie jumped up and down in excitement. "Let's hurry up and dig!" she exclaimed. "I brought my sand shovel. I'll get it."

She ran off and soon returned with a toy shovel.

Nancy, Bess, and George were amused at the thought of digging for hidden pirate treasure with this implement.

The bald bather had walked up, curious to see what was going on. When he realized that they were planning to dig with the toy shovel, he said, "I have a spade in my trunk and would be glad to lend it to you."

He hurried to his parked car and returned a few minutes later with the spade. He handed it to Bess and looked at her with an admiring smile. It made her blush.

"Thank you," she said and pushed the spade into the sand. She worked for a while. Then, when the hole was about a foot deep, she handed the spade to Nancy.

"Your turn," she declared.

While the day-camp children, Mrs. Turnbull, and the bald-headed man watched, Nancy continued to dig. When her arms got tired, she looked at George.

"You're next if I don't hit something," she said, and shoved the spade down once more. There was a slight clang of metal against metal. Nancy exclaimed, "I hit something hard!"

"It must be the treasure!" Tessie cried out, jumping up and down.

# CHAPTER XIII

## *Doubloons!*

NANCY lifted Tessie into the hole, and she dug the objects out with her toy shovel. As she handed up a battered tin knife and spoon, she squealed in delight. "Did pirates leave these?"

"I don't know," Nancy replied.

"They could have been utensils dropped by a picnicker and buried in the sand," George pointed out.

Bess examined the pieces carefully. "I'm sure they're very old," she said. "They're probably from a pirate ship."

"Can I keep them?" Tessie begged.

"Maybe," Nancy replied.

Tessie looked for more treasure, but reported that there was nothing. Nancy helped her climb out, then offered to dig deeper. A few minutes later, she stopped suddenly and stepped out.

"Tessie, go down and feel around in the sand."

In a few seconds the little girl handed up a coin. Nancy looked at it and exclaimed, "This is a doubloon! A Spanish doubloon!"

Tessie wanted to know what a doubloon was. Bess explained that many years ago Spanish ships sailed across the ocean to Mexico, which was not far from Florida.

"They captured people and had them do all sorts of work. One thing was to make coins like those they had in Spain. They were called doubloons and were made of pure gold."

Tessie tried to dig farther, but found it impossible. She had hit solid coral rock. The little girl looked up at Nancy and said, "Please lift me out and then you dig."

Nancy complied. She assumed that the coral rock had been there a long time, but suspected that something precious might have been buried before the tiny polyps had built their pile of rock on top of it.

She chipped at the coral with the spade, and presently saw a few more doubloons. She handed them up to Tessie, then Nancy broke off more of the rock. In a few moments she climbed out of the hole, but helped Tessie down.

This time the little girl exclaimed, "Oh, I found a bracelet!" and climbed out.

Nancy explained that all treasure found must be taken to police headquarters and listed. "You can't keep everything you find," she added. "It's against the law."

*Nancy exclaimed, "It's a Spanish doubloon!"*

George scraped the hole thoroughly, but found nothing more, and came back up.

"Now I suppose we must put all that sand back," Bess said with a sigh.

"Of course," George replied. "Otherwise some-one could fall in and get hurt. Here, my dear cou-sin, you haven't been digging for a while. You start."

Bess did not look very happy, and the bald-headed man stepped up. "Don't worry, I'll do it for you," he offered, and took the spade.

With powerful arms he threw the sand back into the hole and soon the beach looked just as it had before.

"Thanks," Bess said. "That was very nice of you."

"Don't mention it. Want an ice cream?"

"Oh—no, thanks. I—I'm on a diet."

The man smiled and left to take his spade back to the car.

George chuckled. "How come you're turning down food?"

Bess blushed. "As I said, I'm on a diet!"

George and Nancy laughed. "Best joke I've heard in years!" George exclaimed. "If he had been young and handsome, Bess would have eaten three banana splits!"

Mrs. Turnbull's children became restless now that the treasure hunt was over and asked if they could have their lunch. The woman nodded and again thanked Nancy for rescuing Tessie. She promised to take the treasure to the authorities on their way home, then beckoned her charges toward the grove. The children waved good-by and followed the woman.

After they had gone, Nancy said, "I'm sure someone else found the rest of that treasure."

"I hope he reported it," George said, grinning.

The three friends walked along the beach.

"From Mrs. Cosgrove's description," Nancy said, "this should be the way to the old lighthouse."

"You're right," George confirmed a few seconds later, when they saw the building inside a fenced area. It was about sixty feet in height, cone-shaped, and made of brick.

Several other visitors, including a group of boy scouts, had gathered in front of the gate and the girls joined them. "The tour will begin in a few minutes," the scoutmaster told them.

He had hardly finished speaking, when an attractive young woman in a ranger's uniform unlocked the gate. She admitted the visitors and led them around the lighthouse toward the water. They went up to a small porch and gathered around her as she talked about the building's history.

"This lighthouse hasn't been used for years," she said, "because others have been built farther out in the bay. However, it has an interesting background. This building is not the original one."

"What happened to that one?" a scout asked.

"It was burned."

"Was anyone in it?"

"Unfortunately, yes. The lighthouse keeper John Thompson and his black assistant. It was dangerous living out here at that time because the Indians who occupied this territory were not friendly. Many of the Seminoles had had their wives and children taken away by white people, who made them slaves. Naturally they were furious and did everything they could to retaliate.

"One night a crowd of Indians came here. A circular stairway led to the top, where the great lantern was. The Seminoles set the old wooden building on fire to prevent the keeper and his assistant from escaping. The two men hid in the tower, but bullets whizzed at them continuously. The black man was shot and died, and the keeper was wounded. But the fire attracted the attention of two ships offshore."

"Did anyone come to rescue them?" Bess asked anxiously.

"Yes, but meanwhile John Thompson rolled a keg of powder down the stairway. When it hit the fire below, the powder exploded and the Indians ran for their lives!"

"Good!" a boy scout exclaimed. "But did Mr. Thompson get saved?"

"Yes, but the rescuers almost failed. When the ships got closer to the lighthouse, they sent out a lifeboat, but the crew realized that it would be impossible to climb to the top of the tower. Instead, they tried sending out a kite from which there was a stout cord for Mr. Thompson to grab. Unfortunately he wasn't able to, so they tied the twine to a ramrod and fired it from a musket. This time Thompson grabbed the cord and used it to haul up heavier rope. On it two men climbed to the tower room to take care of him. He reached the ground safely."

"I'm glad to hear that," Bess said.

"The black man was buried," the ranger went on, "but I've never seen his grave. It was unmarked so the Indians couldn't find it."

She let the visitors inside the lighthouse, which had been modernized and had an upstairs bedroom. After they had inspected the sparse but comfortable furnishings, they went down again and walked outside.

"I want to show you some of the bushes around here," the ranger said, pointing to a shrub. "This is called an inkberry bush. It was used by the Indians and the early settlers of the area to write letters with."

"How?" one of the boy scouts wanted to know.

"The liquid from its berries is just like ink," the ranger replied. From a little basket that she carried on her wrist, she took a number of small plastic bags. Each contained an inkberry. She handed them out to the visitors as souvenirs.

"These berries were also used to make a dye," she explained. "When you get home, try to write with the ink."

The boy scouts giggled. "On regular paper?"

"Sure. White paper, yellow paper. You can even use a paper bag."

Next the young woman pointed out a bush called sea grape. "This yields fruit to make jelly," she said. "But notice the leaves. They are very thick, and you can write on them." She took one off the bush, picked up a small stick from the ground, and wrote:

> *Thank you for coming.*
> *I hope you had a good time.*

Then she handed the leaf to the scoutmaster. He passed it on to his charges and thanked her for the interesting tour. Now she opened the gate and the visitors said good-by.

When the girls were back in their car, George grinned. "I'll remember that sea-grape bush. If I'm ever in a tight spot out on the water, I'll write a message on one of them and let it float ashore."

Nancy laughed. "You may have to wait twenty years before someone picks it up!"

The girls drove back to Key Biscayne, chatting about their experiences on Cape Florida. When they reached the business district, traffic became congested and momentarily stopped.

Nancy watched the scene in front of her and suddenly gasped. "Bess! George!" she said. "Do you see those two men getting into that red car up ahead?"

"I see them," George said. "They look like Matt Carmen and Breck Tobin!"

"Right!" Bess agreed. "What are we going to do?"

Just then traffic began to move again. The suspects started their red sedan and pulled in a few cars ahead of the girls.

"Let's chase them!" George urged.

"Yes," Nancy said. "Only right now it's a rather slow chase."

At the next big intersection their quarry turned right. The girls followed and kept the sedan in sight. Soon the traffic thinned out and Nancy sped after the two suspects!

# CHAPTER XIV

## *Periscope Pursuit*

THE driver of the car Nancy was pursuing seemed to be aware that he was being followed. Not only did he put on speed, but he turned corners with squealing wheels. Nancy and her friends were convinced that the men were indeed Carmen and Tobin.

Bess, who was tossed violently from side to side in the rear seat, begged Nancy to slow down. "Please don't go so fast! We'll overturn!"

"Sorry," Nancy replied, then grinned. "This time those men are afraid of us. A sure sign of guilt. They don't want us to alert the town cops."

They reached an intersecting highway, and the men drove onto it. They were getting ahead of the girls and it was obvious that they had no intention of obeying the speed limit.

"They're worried about being caught," George said. "On the other hand, I'm sure they wouldn't want to be stopped by the police to show their licenses. That would be a dead giveaway."

Nancy did not want to disobey the traffic laws, but how else was she going to catch the two suspects? She gave her car more power and it raced along the highway.

George remarked, "If we could only get close enough to see the license number, we could report those men to the police instead of chasing them."

Nancy agreed and asked, "Did you notice anything on the license plate?"

"Only that it was from Connecticut," George answered. "Maybe the car was stolen, and that's one reason why they want to get away in such a hurry."

The words were hardly out of George's mouth, when the girls heard a siren behind them.

"Oh, oh!" Bess said, worried.

Obediently Nancy drove to the side of the road and waited for the police car to pull alongside her. An officer jumped out and walked up to the girls.

"You're going over seventy in a fifty-five mile zone," he grumbled. "What's the idea?"

"We're chasing a car,' Nancy said. "But now we've lost it. We believe one of the passengers is wanted by the Navy for going AWOL. His name is Giuseppe Matthews, but he's known under the alias of Matt Carmen or Breck Tobin.

"How do you know about all this?"

"He owns a boat called *The Whisper* and has been harassing us in Biscayne Bay. Yesterday we were at the Naval Office and saw a picture of him. You can check with Captain Smith."

The officer hesitated a moment, then said, "What did the car look like?"

"It was a red sedan with a Connecticut license plate," George put in.

"All right. I'll take care of the matter and send out an alarm. Since you were trying to do a good deed, I won't give you a ticket this time. But from now on, leave chasing criminals to the police."

Nancy nodded. "It's just that he turned up ahead of us in the downtown traffic," she said.

"I understand. And thanks for the information."

The officer said good-by and went back to his car. Nancy pulled out onto the highway again and to the surprise of Bess and George did not head home. Instead she went toward the waterfront.

"Where are you going?" Bess asked.

"If the two men were Breck Tobin and Matt Carmen, they're probably headed for *The Whisper.*"

"Right. But what makes you think we'll catch up with them? They're way ahead of us by now."

"True. On the other hand, if they suspect we

tipped off the police, they may change their minds and not go to their boat. We may be able to find *The Whisper* at a dock," Nancy reasoned.

"Pretty smart," Bess agreed. "Let's go!"

The young sleuths drove as close to the water's edge as they could, then got out of the car and walked. They looked for a red sedan, as well as *The Whisper*. After carefully scanning all the boats and parking areas, without finding either they gave up.

"I'll bet they took the boat and skipped to Crocodile Island," George said. "They probably parked the car in some garage."

"Well, it was a good try," Bess added.

Nancy drove to the Cosgrove house. Their hosts were not there. The telephone was ringing so Nancy answered it. The caller was Colombo.

"Oh, hello," Nancy said. "How are things going for you?"

"Very fine," the young man replied. "I like my work, and the people at the club are very good to me."

"Have you heard any news from Crocodile Island?"

"Yes, I have," Colombo answered. "A worrisome piece of news. My friend Sol there got a message through to me at the YMCA. He advised me to get out as fast as I could, since Gimler had found out I was staying there and threatened to have me arrested."

"Oh, dear," Nancy said. "I'm sorry to hear you've been tracked down. Have you any idea how Gimler knew?"

"No. But I took Sol's advice and moved out right away. If you have a pencil and paper handy, I'll give you my new address and phone number."

"Good. Hold on just a minute."

When Nancy returned with a note pad, he dictated the information. Then she asked him, "Colombo, did you ever see a submarine near Crocodile Island?"

"A submarine? No. But it's strange you should ask. Sol mentioned once that he'd seen a periscope. But the sub never surfaced while he was watching, so I thought he'd mistaken something else for a periscope."

"Has Sol told you anything else?" Nancy asked.

"Yes. He overheard Gimler say to one of the workmen that he wanted no more visitors on Crocodile Island until he gave the word. He said something like 'People are too inquisitive, and not about crocodiles, either.' "

Nancy thanked Colombo for the information and then said to him, "You'd better be careful."

"I will," he promised.

Nancy reported the conversation to Bess and George, and added, "I have a strong hunch that the crocodile farm is a cover-up for some bigger operation. I wish I knew what it was."

Bess spoke up. "Do you think it involves that big pine box we saw lowered from the freighter?"

"Probably," Nancy replied. "The freighter, *The Whisper,* and the submarine are all part of it, I'm sure."

"If you're right," George said, "what do we do next?"

"Tomorrow, let's see if we can locate the periscope and try to follow the sub," Nancy suggested.

"What!" Bess exclaimed. "If you're going on another wild-goose chase, count me out!"

"Okay," said George, "we'll leave the chicken at home. If you prefer that to a great adventure, you can have it. Nancy, I like your plan. I suppose our going will depend on the tide. When Danny comes home, let's ask him."

Nancy nodded. "Also, we'll have to find out if the *Pirate* has been repaired."

Bess laughed. "I see there's no holding you back. And you know perfectly well I don't want to be thought of as a chicken. We'll all go."

"Thank goodness!" George said. "I was just beginning to think I'd have to put you in a coop."

Bess made a face at her cousin, then she changed the subject. "Here comes Danny. Let's ask him about his boat."

The young man said he was happy to tell them that the *Pirate* was in good running order once more. "I'll look up the tide table," he said. When he returned, Danny announced that morning would be the best time to go. "Are you game to get up real early?"

"Sure," the girls chorused.

By six-thirty they were seated in the skiff. Danny put on full speed and the *Pirate* bounced across the water-covered sand dunes. When they reached the green channel alongside Crocodile Island, Nancy picked up the binoculars and stared ahead.

Suddenly a broad grin appeared on her face. "I see it!" she exclaimed.

In the distance she had discovered the periscope. It seemed to be motionless. The sub evidently was lying in the channel.

Nancy asked Danny to race toward it as fast as he could. They had barely started, however, when the periscope disappeared.

"The sub is taking off!" George exclaimed. "Oh, I hope we can catch it!"

Danny followed the green waterway into the ocean. The elusive periscope had not appeared again, and the young people assumed that the sub was now in deeper water.

"Oh, hypers!" George cried out, using one of her favorite expressions. "Now we've lost it! Where did it go?"

They all knew it was futile to search in the wide expanse of ocean. The only possible way to

spot the sub would be from a plane or a helicopter.

"We'd better turn back," Danny suggested.
"It's a long way home, and I'm afraid we'll have
to run for it to make Biscayne Bay before low
tide."

He entered the channel again, putting on full
speed. But when he turned into the shallow water
beyond Crocodile Island he looked worried.

"Do you think we'll make it?" George asked
him.

"I'll do my best," he said grimly.

There was no more conversation as the skiff
fairly flew on top of the water. Everything went
well until they were about halfway home. Danny,
who had been turning left and right to avoid the
higher dunes, suddenly swerved very hard. He
straightened the boat again, but within seconds
it rammed into a long sandbank. The motor
churned desperately for a moment, then stopped.

The impact had knocked all three girls from
their chairs. They flew through the air and
landed with a resounding splash in the water!

# CHAPTER XV

## *Jungle Attack*

DRENCHED with seawater and covered with sand, Nancy, Bess, and George stood up alongside the *Pirate*. To Danny's amazement they were not angry. Instead, they started to laugh. George said, "Thanks for the unexpected bath!"

Bess, looking at the skiff, remarked, "I guess we'll have to walk home."

"Or wait for high tide," Danny told her. "Instead of waiting, however, you could walk to that key over there and investigate the wildlife. It isn't far from here."

"Does anyone live on it?" Nancy asked.

"No, it's uninhabited."

Bess chose to stay with Danny and dry out in the hot sun, but Nancy and George were interested in seeing the key, so they sloshed through the shallow water to the mangrove-lined island.

When the girls reached it, they scrambled over

roots and coral rocks. There was nothing to see but bushes and trees.

"It's a real jungle!" George said.

"I'll say it is," Nancy agreed. "Look over at that mangrove." She pointed.

George stared in amazement. A fish was climbing up the bark!

The two girls watched to see how high it would go. To their astonishment it disappeared in the leafy foliage above.

"This place is absolutely spooky!" George muttered.

She had barely finished the sentence when they heard a dog barking.

"There must be somebody on this key besides us," Nancy said. "But let's go on. Maybe we'll see something else unique."

The dog's barks were coming closer, and the girls wondered if he were friendly. If not, both of them would have to scramble up the next tree!

They waited for the animal to come closer. When it did, Nancy gasped. He was an Irish terrier, and on his right forepaw were six toes!

"E-fee!" Nancy cried out, recognizing the animal from Crocodile Island. "How did you get here?"

The dog came up to the girls at once, wagged his tail in delight, and barked in short yaps.

"Is your master around?" Nancy asked apprehensively.

The girls stood still, waiting for someone to appear. But no one did. The dog stayed close by, and acted so glad to see them that they were convinced there were no other human beings on the small key besides themselves.

George asked, "Do you suppose someone from Crocodile Island left E-fee here on purpose?"

Nancy shrugged. "If so, it's a pretty poor way to treat the dog. He couldn't swim back to Crocodile Island. It's too far from here."

Puzzled, Nancy and George walked on. E-fee bounded ahead of them. Presently he ran to a little clearing and began to bark frantically. The girls hurried to the spot where he was standing.

E-fee looked up at them, gave a few quick barks, then dug furiously into the sandy soil.

"Nancy, he's looking for something," George said. "Maybe his master is buried here!"

"Horror stories again, eh?" Nancy quipped. But she felt apprehensive herself.

E-fee did not stop digging until he had made a good-sized hole. Then he looked at the girls as if to say, "Go ahead. Take a look!"

Nancy and George stepped forward and gazed into the hole. To their amazement a pistol lay inside!

"Where did that come from?" George asked. "Do you suppose E-fee's master put it there, and then went away, leaving the dog to guard it?"

Nancy thought a moment, then said, "It's a good guess, George. Perhaps the men on Crocodile Island didn't want E-fee there anymore because his barks attracted too much attention. Now that the island is closed to the public, I'd say they don't want a dog calling attention to the place if something illegal is going on there."

George got down on her knees and carefully lifted the pistol out of the hole. She examined it and found that the firearm was not loaded, and the serial number on it had been almost obliterated.

"Let's take it along," she suggested. "If nobody owns this island and a person comes here and buries a weapon, then it becomes the property of the finder."

Nancy smiled. "I love your logic. We'll take the pistol with us, but we'll turn it over to the police."

The girls filled up the hole, shoving the sandy soil in place with their shoes. Then they went on exploring. Nancy and George watched for anyone who might be on the island. E-fee followed. Since he did not bark, they felt reasonably sure they were alone.

Presently Nancy noticed that there were many twelve inch lizards running around. Some hid in the undergrowth, but a large number of them were at a fresh-water pond containing hundreds of mosquito larvae. The lizards were eating them greedily.

The girls were so busy watching the fascinating sight that they failed to notice a swarm of mosquitoes coming their way. Suddenly the mosquitoes enveloped Nancy and George, biting furiously! As the girls tried to duck, the insects sang, divebombed, and stung them.

"Oh, dear!" George cried out. "We'd better get away from here fast!"

With E-fee at their heels, the girls ran as quickly as they could. To their dismay the mosquitoes followed!

"This is awful!" George panted. "A real jungle attack. What'll we do?"

"I've heard," Nancy called out, "that the only way to get rid of these pests is to dive into the water."

The two friends hurried toward the spot where they had entered the key. The going was rough. Despite the protection of their shoes they nicked their ankles on coral rocks and tripped on tree roots, which made them wince in pain. The mosquitoes kept buzzing around their heads, necks, arms, and legs, which were fast covered with bites.

The dog had long since outdistanced them and met the girls among the mangroves along the shore. When he saw them dive into the water, which was now deeper, he ran in after them. How good the cool water felt!

Nancy and George swam all the way to the *Pirate*. E-fee followed. When they reached the skiff and stood up, Bess exclaimed, "What in the world happened to you, and where did this dog come from?"

Without being invited, E-fee climbed aboard. Nancy said, "He's a visitor from Crocodile Island."

George explained about the jungle attack of mosquitoes, and how they had found the dog.

"Jump in, girls," Danny said. "I have just the thing for you."

He opened the first-aid kit and gave each girl an antihistamine pill, followed by a drink of water. Then he handed them a tube of medicine and suggested that they lather themselves with it.

They did this and soon the medication began to take effect, making them feel better.

"What an experience!" Bess said. "Tell us the rest of the story."

"We think someone from Crocodile Island buried a pistol there and then left E-fee behind."

"How did you know that?" Danny asked.

"Here's proof." George said, and pulled the pistol out of her pocket.

"What!" Bess shrank back in surprise. "Where on earth—"

"It was buried on the key," George explained. "E-fee dug it up. Since he knew where it was, we figure he saw his master bury it. We brought the pistol to give to the authorities."

"Is—is it loaded?" Bess asked, uncomfortable at the thought.

"Relax. It's empty," George said.

Danny asked whether they intended to return the dog to his master. At once George answered, "Not on your life! I'll find a nice home for him."

Danny said he was glad to hear this because he felt it would be unwise to keep the animal at the Cosgrove home. "Some of your enemies might track it down, and then we'll be in trouble. You might be accused of stealing E-fee!"

"I agree," Nancy said. "Do you think we should drop him off at the animal shelter?"

"That's a good idea," Danny replied.

Nancy now asked, "How about those mosquitoes? We have never seen a swarm like that before."

"In Key Biscayne and other inhabited keys they have mosquito control, which takes care of the problem. The insects breed only in deserted little islands like the one you were on. Lizards act as natural balancers."

George remarked, "If they eat that whole swarm, they're sure to have indigestion!"

The others laughed, then Danny said, "Usually mosquitoes are bothersome only during the rainy season. I didn't think you'd encounter any at this time of year."

"All right, we forgive you." George grinned.

"Thanks." Danny now asked, "Do you want to go periscope hunting again or do a little more sightseeing?"

"Neither!" Nancy said quickly. "All I want is a shower and some more of that soothing lotion."

"I second the motion," George added. "Let's head for home."

After the group docked in Key Biscayne, they brought E-fee to the animal shelter. The girls felt bad about leaving him, but just then a woman and her little girl stopped and asked if they were looking for a home for the dog.

"Yes," Nancy replied.

The child was already patting the dog, whose tail was wagging happily. The little girl looked up. "Mommy, can't we take this one? I love him already."

The woman smiled and said to Nancy, "Is he gentle?"

"Oh, very, and a good watch dog."

The little girl gave E-fee a tremendous hug. Her mother said to the man in charge of the shelter, "We'll take E-fee and give him a good home. By the way, what does his name mean?"

"Dog—in Seminole," Bess answered, and the little girl giggled.

Nancy, Bess, and George left the shelter, happy

that E-fee would be living with kind people instead of suspected criminals.

Their next stop was police headquarters, where George turned in the pistol and explained where it had come from. An officer dusted it for fingerprints while they waited, but unfortunately there were none except George's.

"It'll be difficult to trace the owner," the officer told them, "unless we can find a bullet fired from this gun." He thanked the young people for bringing the weapon in. Then they left.

"And now into the tub!" George said gleefully when they reached the Cosgrove home.

"After I take a shower," Nancy said, "I'll be ready for another bit of sleuthing. I'd like to see a submarine. Danny, do you think there might be one in port at the Key West Naval Base?"

"It's possible," he replied. "I don't know if they'll let you go aboard, though."

"We can try. If we tell them about the mysterious periscope at Crocodile Island, they might."

George chuckled. "Of course they will. How could anyone ever say no to Nancy Drew?"

# CHAPTER XVI

## *Exciting Phone Call*

AFTER the girls had bathed and changed into fresh clothes, they went into the living room and told their hosts about the adventure on the uninhabited island.

Mrs. Cosgrove was worried about the pistol, but Danny calmed his mother by telling her that they had already delivered it to the police.

Nancy said, "I'd like to learn more about submarines. Mr. Cosgrove, do you know someone at the naval base in Key West?"

He nodded. "As usual, you're lucky. It happens that Captain Townsend is an old friend of mine. I'll give you a letter of introduction and if he can spare the time, I'm sure he'll show you around and answer all your questions." He smiled at Nancy. "But don't ask him to tell you any of the secrets of the U. S. Navy!"

Nancy knew she was being teased because of

her reputation as a girl sleuth. She smiled back and said, "Maybe I'll find out some secrets without being told!"

Danny called across the room, "I dare you to!"

After breakfast the following morning Mr. Cosgrove wrote the letter of introduction to Captain Townsend. "Take this to his house on the base," he said.

Danny asked to be excused from the trip, because of a dentist's appointment, so the three girls drove off by themselves. When they reached the Naval Station at Key West, they were amazed at the immensity of it. Two sailors guarded the entrance gate and asked for the visitors' identification. Nancy pulled out the letter from Mr. Cosgrove and showed it to them.

"Go ahead," one of the sailors said. "Take a right turn and at the next street ask someone where Captain Townsend's house is."

They followed the directions and in a few minutes pulled up to an attractive bungalow. Many varieties of flowers were in full bloom in the front yard.

Nancy parked and the girls walked to the door. They were admitted by another sailor, who took them to Captain Townsend's office in his home. Nancy showed him the letter.

"So you're a friend of the Cosgroves?" he asked. "Our families have been very close for many years. Please sit down."

The girls seated themselves in the comfortable wicker furniture. Then the captain asked what he could do for them.

Nancy said she would love to look around the base. "But before that, I want to ask you an important question."

She related the story of having seen a periscope in the green waterway at Crocodile Island. "But each time our skiff approaches it, the periscope disappears quickly. Do you know of any sub in that area?"

Captain Townsend shook his head. "No. But let me make a quick call and see if there's any record of it."

He punched a number into his desk phone and in a few minutes had his answer. "There's no record of any sub plying those waters. Are you sure you didn't mistake a mischievous coot for a periscope?"

"You mean those little black birds that stay underwater with just their long necks and heads showing?"

"Yes."

Up to this point George had not spoken. Now she exclaimed indignantly, "Nancy and the rest of us would certainly know the difference between a coot and a periscope!"

Captain Townsend laughed. "No offense meant. I'm sorry I can't help you."

"Perhaps you can help us with another sub,"

Nancy said. "I'd like to see one. Are there any in port?"

"You came at a good time," Captain Townsend said. "I'm going off duty just about now, so I'll be glad to give you a personally conducted tour of the base and show you a sub."

"Oh, that's great!" Nancy exclaimed. "Thank you."

The officer stood up and led them outside. "I don't have a car here, so shall we take yours?" he asked Nancy.

"Of course," she said, and handed him the keys.

He climbed behind the wheel and drove the girls up and down the various streets of the base, pointing out office buildings, barracks, recreation centers, and the air station.

Nancy was fascinated by the very high antenna. Captain Townsend said, "From here we can send messages to every part of the world."

"By satellite?" George asked.

"Yes."

They passed the base's hospital and came to an area where helicopters were parked.

"The men who fly these birds are specially trained in antisubmarine work," the captain explained. "They survey suspicious areas and try to spot invading enemy subs."

Bess spoke. "Maybe one of them should make a run over to Crocodile Island."

"I'll see to it," the captain promised. "It would only take a few minutes." Then he teased, "But that periscope you saw had better be there!"

They passed a building where students learned how to read sonar, and another containing advanced undersea weaponry, which was used as a teaching facility for the naval personnel.

"We have a great course here in underwater swimming and diving," the officer stated. "Some of the men later go into deep-sea diving work. You've probably seen pictures of them on television."

All the girls said they had and were fascinated by the sea life the pictures showed.

Bess commented, "But some of those creatures are too dangerous for me!"

The captain laughed. Then Nancy asked if by any chance there was a nuclear submarine in port.

"No, there isn't," he replied. "Just one of the older types. Would you like to go into it and have a look?"

"I'd love to," Nancy replied, and George and Bess wanted to, also.

When they reached it, a sailor standing on the deck saluted his superior officer. Captain Townsend offered to show the girls the interior.

The hatch was open and he led the way down the iron ladder to the deck below. As the girls gazed ahead, they noticed a long, narrow, center passageway.

George remarked, "I never saw so many things in such a tiny space. This is like a small apartment with a whole crew living in it!"

"And everything is so neat!" Bess added. "If I could keep my room like this, my mother would be very happy."

Nancy was interested in the crews' quarters. One bunk was perched high above a tremendous black tube. As Captain Townsend saw her eyeing it, he asked, "How would you like to sleep on top of a torpedo?"

"I wouldn't!" she replied.

The "kitchen" intrigued Bess. Every inch of the galley was used, and the equipment, including stove and refrigerator, was so compact that it amazed the visitors. She asked how many men could be served from such small quarters.

"Of course that depends on the size of the sub," the captain replied. "I think this one carries a complement of about thirty men."

As the visitors proceeded, Nancy inquired about the many upright lockers. "What is kept in them?"

Captain Townsend opened one. It was full of coiled rope, most of it hanging on hooks.

Another sailor's locker held work clothes. Nancy could see several M-16 rifles in slots behind the clothing. She wondered why they were on a sub that used only torpedoes. "Perhaps the men carry them when they're on land," she thought.

The officer said that the sub contained a ship-to-shore telephone. "Nancy, would you like to call someone?"

"Oh, yes," she replied. "I'll phone Mr. Cosgrove. Maybe you'd like to speak to him."

The captain placed the call and spoke to his old friend, then he handed the instrument to Nancy. Mr. Cosgrove said, "An important call came for you."

"Oh!" she said. "From home?"

"No, from your friend Ned Nickerson." Nancy could feel her face reddening. "He and Burt and Dave would like to come down here and see you. Ned said he'd call again for an answer. Mrs. Cosgrove and I would be happy to have them stay with us."

Bess and George were excited by the news. It would be such fun to see the boys again!

Captain Townsend said they must leave now as it was time for the crewmen to return and go through a drill.

The visitors climbed topside and went to the car. After the girls had thanked the captain profusely and left him at his home, Nancy drove off.

On the way to the Cosgroves, she said, "I have an idea. How about the boys staying with Mr. Gonzales instead of at the Cosgroves? Gimler and Sacco don't know them, so Ned, Burt, and Dave might pick up some good tips."

The other girls liked the idea, so Nancy drove to Mr. Gonzales's club. They all walked inside.

The man at the desk recognized Nancy and said, "Miss Boonton, are you looking for Mr. Gonzales?"

"Yes, I am," she replied. "Is he here?"

Fortunately Mr. Gonzales was there. He came to meet Nancy. She introduced the other girls, then asked him, "How would you like a three-man bodyguard?"

Mr. Gonzales burst into laughter. "Is it that bad? Have you uncovered some new evidence?"

Nancy explained why she had made the request, and he accepted her suggestion that the three boys stay with him.

"Now that you girls will have some escorts, how would you like to come to the Saturday night dinner-dance here?" Mr. Gonzales asked. "The food is always excellent, and the music exactly what you like."

"We'd love to accept," Nancy said.

The man looked at her and teased, "Don't get yourself involved in some fix related to the mystery of Crocodile Island so you can't get here."

"I'll do my best," Nancy promised, grinning.

As she was about to drive out of the club grounds, Nancy saw Colombo. He apparently was headed for a bus. She stopped the car and called to him.

"Would you like a ride into town?" she asked.

"Indeed I would," Colombo replied. "Thank you so much." He opened the door to the rear seat and stepped in. "I'm glad I met you. I just received a phone call from my friend Sol. He wants me to meet him at a garage. He sounded excited."

"He didn't say why?" Nancy asked.

"No. When we get to the garage, why don't you girls wait outside? I'll go in and talk to Sol. He may have some important news from Crocodile Island."

# CHAPTER XVII

## *Deadly Golf Ball*

IN a few minutes Colombo brought his friend Sol outside and introduced him. To start a conversation Nancy asked him how he had managed to come to Key Biscayne from Crocodile Island.

The broad-shouldered, dark-skinned man replied, "I begged for a ride with a sightseer who wasn't allowed to land. I waded out into the water and asked him to bring me to town. I was glad he didn't ask me why sightseers were not allowed to see the reptiles that day, so I didn't have to say anything. I hate to go back, but I need the money."

Colombo asked him how he planned to return.

"I'll hire a boat and pilot to take me out there after dark. Meanwhile I want to have a good time here. You know, it's pretty dull in that place."

Colombo said, "I know. Sol, I've told you these girls are detectives. Tell them your latest news."

Sol nodded. "I think you know a good deal

already. But if you can solve the latest mystery of Crocodile Island, you'll put Mr. Gimler and Mr. Sacco to shame. There's no doubt that they're covering up something big."

Nancy asked him if he knew what it was, but Sol shook his head. "I overheard the bosses bragging about the huge amount of money they were making. I know very well it's not from selling crocodiles to zoos and animal parks."

Colombo suggested that maybe there were some under-the-table sales, which Sol knew nothing about.

"There could be," his friend replied. "But I see the company's books, and I'm sure they report every sale of crocodiles faithfully."

Nancy was puzzled, and asked about *The Whisper's* comings and goings. Sol knew little. "Mr. Gimler often goes out in it, but he never says where. Sometimes he brings back food."

Bess remarked that it sounded secretive. "I guess Mr. Gimler doesn't want anybody finding out what's going on at the island."

Sol agreed. "By the way, those of us who are still working there are likely to lose our jobs any time."

"Why?" Nancy asked.

Sol said he had overheard the bosses say that they planned to sell out. They were going to offer all their shares of stock to Mr. Gonzales or some other people.

"That's strange," Nancy reflected. "Not long

ago Mr. Gimler and Mr. Sacco were offering to buy Mr. Gonzales's stock in the Crocodile Ecology Company."

No one had an answer to this puzzle. Sol changed the subject. "Whether I lose my job or not, I'd like to get away from that place. It scares me. I have a feeling that the police are going to find out that something crooked is going on at the island and arrest the top men. Then I'll be called in as a witness. Mr. Gimler and Mr. Sacco might even tell lies about me and I'll be sent to jail!"

Nancy was shocked to hear this. "You mean that the partners are really mean and mad enough to do that?"

"I wouldn't put it past them," Sol replied.

George told him that the girls were only visitors and had very few contacts at Key Biscayne. "But if we ever hear of a job you could fill, we'll let Colombo know."

"Thank you," Sol said. "I'd appreciate it. I don't even like the men I work with out on the island. In fact, I don't trust any of them. If something dishonest is going on, they're probably in league with the bosses."

Nancy said that under the circumstances she was amazed that they had not already discharged Sol. "Unless you haven't given any indication that you're suspicious."

"Oh, I haven't," he told her. "And I don't think the other men have any idea I'm squealing on them."

"That's good," Nancy praised him. "You're sort of playing detective. Keep up the good work and report to us as often as you can."

Sol promised to do so, but said it was becoming more difficult to get away from the island. The few times he had tried it, Gimler had docked his pay.

"That's wicked!" George exclaimed. "Nobody should be expected to stay in one place and work all the time without any recreation!"

After a little more conversation, the girls thanked Sol again and left him and Colombo. As Nancy drove off, Bess asked, "Where to now?"

Nancy said she had a hunch that they should go back to the golf club and report this latest bit of information to Mr. Gonzales. At the desk the girls learned that he was playing golf.

"But he should be back soon," the clerk told them. "Why don't you go out to the porch? From there you can watch him come in on the eighteenth green."

The three friends hurried to the porch and took chairs near the railing. They had a clear view of the green and part of the fairway. Nancy, who played golf well, noticed that there were trees on one side of the fairway just before it ended at the green. "That really makes it hard," she thought. "A person would have to aim a straight shot not to hit those trees."

"Remember that beautiful golf course at the Deer Mountain Hotel, where we solved the mystery of *The Haunted Bridge?*" George asked.

"I sure do," Bess said. "Nancy won a tournament there." She giggled. "Here comes Father Time!"

An elderly man, who was almost as round as he was high and had long white hair and a flowing white beard, putted for the cup, missed it, and made a wry face.

Bess sighed. "This sure is a frustrating game."

"It is," Nancy said. "I've seen people get so mad that they threw their clubs away. Once a fellow almost hit his poor caddy!"

"Here comes Mr. Gonzales," George said. "He's a good distance away from the green. I wonder how he'll make out?"

The girls watched in silence as he took his position behind the ball and swung his club in a few practice strokes. Just as he placed the club behind the ball and got ready for his approach shot, another player's ball whizzed from among the trees to his right and hit him hard on the temple. Mr. Gonzales dropped his club and fell to the ground, unconscious.

"Oh!" all three girls cried out in horror.

Nancy, Bess, and George expected the other player to emerge from the woods and run up to the victim. But no one did.

"That ball must have been sent on purpose to hit Mr. Gonzales!" Nancy exclaimed.

The three girls jumped up and ran toward an outside stairway.

Bess suddenly pointed. "I see somebody running beyond those trees. He's carrying a bag of clubs. He must be the one who shot that ball!"

"Maybe he's a caddy," George added.

Nancy was torn between the desire to hurry after the suspect and the need to help Mr. Gonzales. By the time the girls reached the foot of the stairs, they noticed that several people had surrounded their friend. But no one was taking off after the suspect. This helped Nancy decide what to do, although the man was out of sight.

"Let's go!" she said. "We must catch him!"

"Where do you think he'll run?" Bess asked. "To the caddy house?"

"He doesn't seem to be heading in that direction," George replied. "Maybe he isn't a caddy, but a member who is running scared."

Nancy was already racing across another fairway toward a public road. The man with the golf bag suddenly came into view. He looked back and realized he was being chased. Despite the weight of the bag, he put on extra speed. Before the girls could get to him, he reached the road. A car was waiting for him. He jumped in and it roared off.

"Now we'll never know who he is," Bess wailed.

Nancy said she had seen the license plate and repeated the number to the girls.

"What's more, the glimpse I got of the man makes me think he's the one who spied on us out at the Easton estate!" She added, "Since we can't chase him, let's return to the clubhouse and phone the police."

The girls hurried back and told the manager what they had seen and asked him to call headquarters and give the license number. He did so, and the sergeant on duty promised to send two officers out at once.

While they were waiting, Nancy asked how Mr. Gonzales was. The manager replied, "He's still unconscious, but a doctor is with him. He's in a room down the hall."

Bess decided to go there and see if she could find out anything further. Nancy and George remained in the lobby. When the police officers arrived, the manager introduced them as Parks and Joyce.

"This young lady saw a man with a bag of clubs running away. She'll give you the details," the manager said.

The girl detective described how the suspect had fled in a car, adding that she had managed to see the license plate. "Headquarters has the number."

"Yes, we know it," Parks said. "Can you tell us anything else about the man?"

"Yes," Nancy replied. "I think he's the same person who was spying on me and my friends while we were watching the crocodiles at the Easton estate. He was peering at us from behind some mangroves, so I caught only a glimpse of his face. He had shoulder-length black hair and beady eyes. He might be a half-breed Indian. I'm afraid that's all I can tell you about him."

"That's more than people usually notice," Officer Joyce complimented her. "Thank you for the information."

While he had been talking, Lieutenant Parks picked up the manager's phone and called headquarters. He asked the sergeant on duty to look up the license number Nancy had given him.

"It's urgent," she heard him say.

They all waited for an answer, which came in a few minutes. When the manager heard the name of the owner, he showed utter astonishment. "That's my name! It's my car! It must have been stolen!"

Immediately he called the parking-lot attendant, who phoned back in a few minutes. "Your car is not here! I didn't notice anyone take it. I'm sorry, sir."

The manager hung up. Just then another phone rang. The call was for the officers. Lieutenant Parks picked up the instrument. He said, "That's good. You say the suspects got away?"

The officer put down the phone and reported to his listeners that a few minutes earlier the car had been found abandoned about five miles from the club.

"In that case," Joyce said, "we'll have to depend on this girl's description to nab the fellow.

We're to look for a man with a bag of golf clubs. He has long black hair, beady eyes, and could be a half-breed Indian."

While this conversation had been going on, Bess had been waiting outside the room where Mr. Gonzales was for the doctor to appear. In a few minutes he came outside. She asked how the patient was.

"He has regained consciousness," the physician reported, "but has a racking headache. I've ordered an ambulance to take him to the hospital. No one is to see him, either here or at the hospital."

Bess said thank you, turned, and hurried back to repeat this message to Nancy and George. She heard Lieutenants Parks and Joyce discussing the case. Parks declared that he was sure the suspect would have dumped the golf clubs as soon as possible. As to his being a half breed Indian, there were so many of them around that it would be almost impossible to identify the man they were looking for.

Joyce shrugged. "I guess we're at a dead end on this case."

Nancy spoke. "Maybe not," she said. Then, turning to the manager, she requested, "Will you see if Colombo has returned?"

# CHAPTER XVIII

## Snakes

THE manager, Mr. Burley, learned that Colombo was back and sent for him. He asked him to meet Nancy, Bess, and George in the tropical garden.

"Did something happen?" he questioned, when they met and sat down. He looked worried.

"I'll say it did," George replied. "Mr. Gonzales was hit on the head with a golf ball, which was deliberately aimed at him. It knocked him out and now he's in the hospital."

Colombo stood up, walked in a circle, and spoke Spanish so fast that the girls could not understand him. Finally he sat down again and said, "That is very bad. Please tell me more about it."

Nancy took up the story, and when she finished describing the attacker, Colombo said, "He sounds like a man named Sam Yunki, who used to be a caddy at this club. Then he worked at Crocodile Island a short time. I don't know where he is now."

"When he was at the island," Nancy asked, "was he one of the workmen who was close to Mr. Gimler?"

"Yes, he was. Very close. I'm sure Yunki's the one who threw the golf ball at Mr. Gonzales. He's an excellent shot."

"Did you know him well?" Bess inquired.

"No," Colombo replied. "I was never allowed to be near him."

"That's understandable," George said. "Gimler and his partner wouldn't have wanted you to become a pal of his."

Nancy went into the clubhouse to tell this latest news to Mr. Burley. When she told him about Sam Yunki, he said, "I remember hearing about him. He was surly and uncooperative. That is—unless people paid him handsomely or tipped him generously."

Nancy asked Mr. Burley if he knew that Yunki had worked at Crocodile Island after leaving the club.

"No, I didn't," he said. "I heard he left here unexpectedly and no one knew where he went, not even the other caddies. Well, I'll notify the police at once."

Nancy rejoined her friends, who said Colombo had already gone back to work. As the three girls walked to the parking lot, George said, "We really picked up a good clue!"

When they reached home, their hostess was smiling. "I have another message for you girls," she said. "Nancy, your friend Ned called again. I invited the three boys to come down as soon as they could. It didn't take them long to make up their minds. They'll be at the Miami airport this afternoon."

Nancy gave the woman a hug. "How sweet of you to invite them! You know we wanted to farm them out as bodyguards for Mr. Gonzales, but now he won't need them. He's in the hospital."

"What!" Mrs. Cosgrove cried out in alarm.

Nancy and the girls told her about the day's events.

"Oh, I'm so sorry," Mrs. Cosgrove said. "I hope Mr. Gonzales isn't seriously hurt."

Bess said, "We'll call tomorrow and find out. The doctor said they would need to make some tests."

Nancy, Bess, and George went upstairs to get ready. They gave their hair special attention and put on pretty dresses before going to meet the boys.

Miami airport was crowded, but the girls had no trouble finding the athletes from Emerson College. At once the couples paired off to exchange kisses. Then, while the boys were collecting their baggage and later as they all rode to the Cosgrove home, the girls told them of their adventures to date.

"I'm relieved that you've made such progress in your sleuthing," Ned teased. "We didn't want to come here to join a wild-goose chase."

156 MYSTERY OF CROCODILE ISLAND

George said, "I haven't seen any geese around, but there are crocodiles, alligators, snakes, fish that climb trees—"

"Oh, stop your kidding," Burt interrupted.

"You'll see," George told him.

A few minutes later the young people reached the Cosgrove house. After dinner, Dave said, "Danny, what do you think our chances are of getting onto Crocodile Island? I can't wait to see a crocodile. Nancy told us that recently it has been closed to visitors."

Danny offered, nevertheless, to take them all in the skiff the following morning and try to land on the key. "It may be open," he added cheerfully.

The seven young people set off early and headed directly to Crocodile Island. Nancy suggested that if visitors were allowed ashore, Ned, Burt, and Dave should go without the girls.

"No one there knows you, so you could look around without making the owners suspicious. Perhaps you can pick up some clues we've missed."

Unfortunately the planned visit did not take place. When they reached the island, prominently displayed signs prohibited visitors. Furthermore, there was no activity around the place.

This lack of activity puzzled Nancy. "I can't understand it," she said. "I wonder if something happened."

Danny shrugged. "If we can't go ashore, we

can't find out. Tell you what. Suppose I take you boys to an uninhabited key so you can see exactly what one looks like. The girls haven't seen the island either." He smiled. "I can almost guarantee that you won't find any mosquitoes."

The girls laughed and then told the boys about the jungle attack.

Danny went on to say that the key ahead was reputed to have been a slave hideout. "I mean an Indian-slave hideout."

Ned remarked, "We haven't been here twenty-four hours and I've learned a lot I never knew before."

George grinned. "Oh, hadn't you heard? We three girls and Danny are walking encyclopedias! Just ask us anything you want to know about this place."

"Okay," said Burt. "How deep is the water in Biscayne Bay?"

George did not hesitate a second. "It runs from nothing to twenty feet."

Burt was startled and turned to Danny. "Is she putting us on?"

"No, she's not. George is telling the truth. At low tide some of the sand isn't covered at all. The deep-water channels vary from twelve to thirty feet," he explained.

"Wow!" Burt said. "I never would have guessed. That's interesting."

When they reached the key, Danny stayed in the skiff while the others went ashore. As they scrambled over the mangrove roots, the boys seemed to have trouble.

"This stuff is something!" Dave cried out. "I just turned my ankle."

"You have to get used to it," Bess told him. "And you'd better make sure you don't turn your whole leg!"

The young people found it difficult to walk across the coral rock, mangrove, and spiny plants, which grew in profusion. About quarter of a mile from shore they spotted a tumble-down thatched-roof hut.

Ned remarked, "I thought Danny said this place was uninhabited."

"I'm sure it is," Nancy said. "No one could possibly live in that cabin."

They all struggled up to the hut and stared. Its roof was sagging and the building, made of mangrove branches, was ready to fall apart.

"I've seen enough," Dave announced. "Now I can be a walking encyclopedia myself on the subjects of mangrove trees and coral rocks."

Bess was about to say something, but screamed instead, "Look out!"

"What's the matter?" George asked her.

Bess continued to scream and pointed at the branches of trees over their heads. Large black snakes were falling from them in profusion!

Everyone ran, and the reptiles missed all of them except Ned. One slimy creature landed on

*Snakes were falling from the trees in profusion!*

his shoulders and instantly wound itself around the young man's neck.

"Ugh!" he cried out, trying to pull the snake away.

Burt and Dave jumped to help him. Burt grabbed the snake just behind its head, while Dave closed his fingers around the body near the end of the tail.

Bess was still screaming, with the result that all the other snakes scurried off into the underbrush, apparently frightened.

Within seconds Burt and Dave yanked the reptile from Ned's neck and shoulders. They flung it away, and with swift humping motions, the snake crawled out of sight.

"Thanks, fellows," Ned said. "I'm glad that thing didn't fasten its fangs in my throat!"

Bess's continued screaming had brought Danny dashing through the bushes.

"What happened?" he asked.

George told him, and he said, "Don't worry, Ned. Those snakes are harmless. They live in the water part of the time, but come ashore to hunt for food. I guess they climb the trees to sleep and dry off."

Nancy told Danny his passengers were ready to return to the skiff. After they had reached it and climbed aboard, the boy pointed out a police launch in the distance.

"I wonder where it's going," he said.

Nancy asked, "Isn't that the direction of Crocodile Island?"

"Yes, it is," he replied. "Want to follow it and see what's happening?"

"You bet," everyone replied.

As they neared the crocodile farm they saw the police launch pull up to the pier. Four officers jumped out and went ashore. Nancy and her friends could hear indistinct voices. They assumed the police were ordering everyone on the island to come out of hiding. When no one appeared, the officers blew whistles. At the same time, the men spread out on the island.

"I wish we could do something to help," Nancy said.

Danny suggested that they go around to the other side of the island and see if any of the suspects were trying to escape in a boat. He put on power and presently the *Pirate* was rounding the tip of the key.

"Look!" George exclaimed. "There's a boat and men are climbing into it!"

Nancy and Bess cried out together, *"The Whisper!"*

"Oh, they're getting away!" Bess wailed. "What'll we do to stop them?"

"We should tell the police!" George declared.

# CHAPTER XIX

## *Triple Sleuthing*

"AFTER them!" Burt shouted, and Danny quickly guided the skiff toward the fleeing boat.

*The Whisper* was a more powerful craft, however, and stayed well ahead of them. They followed it through the green waterway and it became smaller and smaller in the distance. By the time they reached the ocean, *The Whisper* was only a tiny dot.

Nancy heaved a sigh. She felt completely defeated. "I was so sure we would close in on those men," she said. "Now they've slipped through our fingers!"

Ned patted her shoulder lightly. "Don't give up," he said kindly. "We're bound to get a break."

George said, "I think the break is coming right now!" She looked into the sky. A helicopter was making its way toward their skiff.

"It's a police helicopter!" Burt pointed out.

The craft lowered until the young people in the skiff could see the officers aboard. They were shouting through a megaphone, but those on the water could not understand a word.

"Too bad we don't have a ship-to-shore or ship-to-ship telephone," Danny said.

The only way Nancy could get a message across to the men above was to point in the direction *The Whisper* had taken. She made motions with her hands to indicate that it was going very fast. Then she put her finger to her lips, hoping the men might translate it to mean "whisper!"

She could see the pilot bobbing his head and assumed he understood what she meant—that they should follow the suspect boat to the ocean. The copter turned and set off in that direction.

Dave spoke up. "Too bad we can't be on hand to witness the capture. I'll bet the men in *The Whisper* put up a real fight."

Bess said, "Well, I for one would just as soon not witness a battle. Let's go back."

The skiff returned to Crocodile Island. The police launch was gone, but two officers stood on the dock and invited the young people to come ashore. They introduced themselves as Patman and Fifer.

"Aren't you Danny Cosgrove and these girls detectives?"

"Yes."

Nancy smiled and said Ned, Burt, and Dave were friends.

"We've made some arrests," Patman reported. "For one, we caught the man named Yunki."

"Oh, the one who hit Mr. Gonzales with a golf ball?" Bess cried out.

"Yes." Putnam said they had found him hiding among some bushes. He had readily confessed to hitting the deadly shot toward Gonzales. But Yunki also said that he had not done it of his own accord. Gimler and Sacco had hired him to do not only this but several other illegal jobs. Yunki was well paid for his dastardly work."

"Where is he now?" Ned asked.

Patman told him that the police launch had taken away Yunki and all the other workers, who admitted helping Gimler and Sacco in some illegal secret work but would not say what it was. Two of the men had escaped, however.

"It's important that we catch them. They're the ones who made phone calls and acted as spies whenever necessary."

"As far as we know, they are still on the island. They are Gimler and Sacco's special henchmen named Stryker and Jackson. Unfortunately for them they were not quick enough to follow Gimler on *The Whisper,* which set off in a hurry when you people showed up at the key."

Nancy asked if Gimler had gone off with Matt Carmen and Breck Tobin. Patman nodded. "Yunki told us that. We sent word for a police helicopter to go out and intercept the craft."

The listening group also learned that the fake

Mr. and Mrs. Cosgrove and their daughter, who had posed as Miss Boonton, had been arrested. They were part of the Gimler-Sacco gang. The weapon E-fee dug up belonged to Sacco, who buried it so the police would not find it if they visited Crocodile Island. He left the dog on the deserted key because E-fee had almost bitten one of the men on *The Whisper*, whose cruelty he hated.

Nancy looked at the police officers and asked, "Did I understand you to say that you think two of the workmen are still on the island?"

"Yes. A couple of Sacco's special buddies, and bad, both of them. They have records."

"Where did they go?" Nancy asked.

"We don't know," Patman replied. He walked off to join his fellow officer in another hunt.

Nancy said to her friends, "Why don't we start a search?"

"Great idea!" Ned agreed.

The others were eager to begin but Bess was cautious. "Maybe the men are armed. If so, we're walking into danger!"

Ned hurried off to ask the officers about the firearms. Patman replied, "According to Yunki they were not armed—didn't have time to go for any. I doubt that you'd be in any danger if you want to look around. Fifer and I must stay within sight of the beach until the launch returns. It took all the captives to jail."

Nancy had followed Ned and was alarmed at

its import. She asked quickly. "Was one of the prisoners a man named Sol?"

Patman pulled a pad from his pocket and consulted it. "I have the list of prisoners here. There's no one named Sol on it."

"I'm glad," Nancy said, "that he's not with Gimler and Sacco. We've talked to him. He's very nice. Probably he didn't come back to the island after being in Key Biscayne."

Nancy and Ned returned to their friends. She suggested that they separate into couples and make their search on the island some distance from one another. We'll be couple one, George and Burt, two; and Bess and Dave, three. In case of trouble call out your numbers instead of your names.

"And, Danny, how about your going around the island in the skiff? If you see anyone or anything suspicious, sound your horn."

"Okay," he agreed.

The three couples started off on their search. Bess and Dave stopped for a few minutes to look at the crocodiles, and Bess remarked, "If all the workers are gone, who's going to take care of these reptiles?"

Dave grinned. "How would you like the job?"

Instead of answering, Bess made a face at him.

Just then one of the old male crocodiles grunted, then hissed, and opened its jaws wide. Within seconds he closed them with such a resounding snap that the couple jumped.

Bess and Dave waited no longer. They took off for a copse of mangroves to start their hunt for the missing suspects.

Meanwhile, Burt and George tramped through a jungle area, looking up into trees, behind bushes, and on the ground. They stopped every few minutes to listen, but everything was quiet and there was no sign anywhere of the wanted men.

They came to a low coral cave and stopped. "Isn't that attractive?" George whispered. "I wonder if those men are hiding inside."

"I'll look," Burt said.

"No! They might trap you and attack!"

"I'll be careful. Just follow me, but wait when I get to the entrance."

The two advanced without making a sound. Slowly they neared the entrance. Then Burt picked up a stone and threw it inside. There was no reaction from within.

He cautiously peered around the rocky opening and saw the small interior. The walls were jagged and arranged in a moon-shaped pattern, but there was no cement or any other indication that the cave was man-made.

"It's empty," Burt reported. "Anyway, it's not much of a hiding place."

George looked inside. "Isn't that coral fascinating?" she said. "Think of the millions of tiny polyps climbing up and dying to form layer after layer of coral."

"Yes," Burt said. "But don't get sidetracked. Never mind the coral now. Let's look for those missing men."

The couple went deeper into the jungle. Rabbits and raccoons scurried away from them. Suddenly the stillness was broken by a loud noise. Something was crashing through the underbrush ahead of them. George wondered if it was an animal. Then they heard human voices.

"They may be the suspects!" Burt whispered. "Come on!"

All this time Nancy and Ned were searching along the waterfront, thinking the men might have hidden a second boat among the mangroves and would try to reach it. Suddenly Nancy stopped short.

"Look!" she said, pointing to a periscope out in the green waterway.

"It's moving in the direction of the island!" Ned said, excited. "Maybe it'll dock here!"

"Let's return to the pier," Nancy suggested.

She and Ned quickly made their way back, careful to remain shielded by trees at all times. Just before they reached the open areas, the submarine surfaced! It slid in noiselessly. The hatch opened, and two men appeared. They jumped to the dock and disappeared in the direction of the main building.

Nancy and Ned wondered if the men were aware of the recent events on the island. Obvi-

TRIPLE SLEUTHING **169**

ously they were not worried about being seen. Or were they just desperate?

Nancy decided on a bold move. "Ned, are you game to go aboard and hide?"

"Sure thing."

"Wait just a second," Nancy said. She plucked a leaf from a trailing sea-grape bush. Next she picked up a small sturdy stick and scratched out the words, "Going aboard. Couple one."

She jabbed the leaf onto a tree twig and beckoned Ned to follow her. Quickly the two went to the open hatch and climbed down the iron ladder.

"Where can we hide?" Ned asked, looking around.

Nancy pointed to the upright lockers and opened one. It contained a coiled rope similar to the one she had seen on the sub in Key West.

Ned checked the adjoining locker. Behind some clothes, many boxes were stacked neatly from the floor to the ceiling. Each one was stamped *High Speed Cameras. Bridgeport, Ct.*

"That's a lot of cameras for a few guys," Ned remarked.

"Right," Nancy said, now suspicious. "Open the next locker."

Ned did, and found similar boxes concealed behind raingear. Further search revealed guns, grenades, and explosives in each locker! Ned shook his head in disbelief, and Nancy's eyes were wide with amazement.

"Ned!" she exclaimed. "Now I know what the secret of Crocodile Island is! Gimler and Sacco are taking expensive high-speed cameras out of the U. S. They're smuggling them to someplace, maybe Mexico!"

As the two hurried back to the ladder, Ned put a hand on Nancy's shoulder. "You're right. And this means we're in great danger. We'd better get out of here before—"

Just then they heard voices. Two men were conversing rapidly and walking toward Nancy and Ned. The couple, who did not want to be seen, scooted into the first two lockers. She hid behind coiled ropes. Ned managed to squeeze in back of the raingear and stood next to the boxes of cameras.

They left the doors slightly ajar so they could see who was coming. The two men they had seen leave the sub, reentered it. Quickly one of them turned a handle, which slowly closed the hatch. The other man rotated a wheel that retracted the periscope. Then he started the engine and the sub moved away.

Nancy and Ned held their breath, wondering what would happen next. The man at the wheel suddenly laughed. He said confidently, "We pulled that one off all right. No more bothering with Gimler and Sacco! Next stop Mexico!

# CHAPTER XX

## Submarine Prisoners

"MEXICO!" Nancy thought.

She and Ned were terrified when they realized that they were being taken out of the country with no chance to call for help. They tried to keep calm and figure out some way to outwit these men.

The prisoners listened attentively when the men resumed their conversation. One said, "I had no idea when we went into shipping stolen cameras with Gimler and Sacco that we could make so much money. I don't know why we ever bothered with the small amount we got out of the Crocodile Ecology Company."

The other man said, "You forget, Williams, that we needed a cover. I'd say we just got out of there in time. That nosey girl detective and her friends are just too smart."

In spite of their predicament, Nancy and Ned smiled at this remark.

Williams said, "Nothing to worry about now, Captain Frederick. We're rid of the bunch."

The men talked about what they were going to do with all the money they had made.

Frederick said, "I'll show those relatives of mine in Mexico what I can do, even if they thought I was a no-good." He laughed raucously. "How easy the whole operation was! We stole a lot of cameras from the factory in Connecticut and bought a whole lot of others cheap on the black market. And sold them at a three hundred percent profit."

Nancy and Ned almost suffocated in the lockers but did not dare miss a word. They learned that the cameras were shipped out at night to a freighter going south. Then they were transferred to *The Whisper,* which carried them to the submarine. Then *The Whisper* returned to the key, which was home base. Whenever the submarine came there, the periscope would be hoisted. If any visitors were on the island, an alarm would be sounded and the sightseers sent away.

Williams said, "It's too bad we couldn't fill that order for five hundred cameras. If the buyer in Mexico had only given us a little more time, we wouldn't have had any trouble."

The men were silent for a while, then Williams said, "We won't be tying up for some time. I think I'll put away this rope we're not using. It's in the way."

He stepped to the locker in which Nancy was

hiding and yanked open the door. The girl detective tried to slump to the floor so she would not be seen, but it was impossible.

Upon spotting her, Williams cried out a volume of expletives. He reached in roughly, grabbed Nancy's arm, and pulled her out into the passageway.

The captain also exclaimed and then said to Nancy, "How did you get here?"

She did not answer.

"I said, how did you come aboard this sub?" the captain demanded.

Still Nancy made no reply.

"I'll make you answer!" Frederick cried out, exasperated, and grabbed hold of her with both arms. He was so strong that she thought he would crush her ribs.

At this second a voice said, "Let her alone!" *Ned!*

The sub's captain let go of Nancy and stared at the young man. "Who are you?"

Ned said nothing. By this time Williams and Frederick were jabbering loudly and arguing with each other about what they should do with their stowaways.

"We can't take them into Mexico!" Williams said.

"You're right," the captain agreed. "What do you suggest? That we go topside, open the hatch, and push them out into the water?"

Ned spoke up. "You'd better not do that," he

said, then decided to try a bluff. "Did you know that we're being followed by helicopters?"

The men looked stunned. Williams rushed to raise the periscope above the water. After turning it in various directions, he said, "I don't see any helicopter."

The captain, angry, yelled at Ned, "You were just trying to bluff us. Well, we're not going to fall for it."

After a pause Williams said, "I have an idea, Captain. We both like money. Why don't we hold these two snoopers for ransom?"

Captain Frederick thought this over and finally agreed it was not a bad idea. "Just how can we work it?" he wondered.

"I'll think of something," his fellow officer said. "Give me time."

Nancy and Ned were glad of the temporary reprieve. Their thoughts went back to Crocodile Island. Where were the rest of their friends? Had they found Nancy's note? If so, had they done anything about it?

All this time the two couples had been very busy. George and Burt had finally startled Stryker and Jackson, who were hiding in the jungle. They managed to corner them, then talked to the men from a distance.

"It's no use to try getting away," George called. "All the others on this island have left. They didn't even wait to take you along. Now you have nothing. They have the money and won't dare come back here because of the police. In fact, there are policemen on the island now, hunting for you."

"What?" Stryker exclaimed, then gave a sneering smile. "You're trying to trick us!"

Burt spoke up. "It's no trick. You don't have a chance."

The couple continued to coax the men to come out of hiding, but several more minutes went by before they consented to do so. Burt told them to walk ahead. He and George would follow.

All the way to the pier on the other side of the island the couple was very watchful in case the men should try to get away. Apparently the fugitives felt beaten because they did not attempt to run or fight.

When the two captives saw the officers on the pier, they knew Burt and George had been telling the truth. The captives raised no objection when they were placed under arrest.

Some time before this, Bess and Dave, having found no trace of the suspects, had started back toward the pier. As they were making their way along the waterfront, Bess grabbed Dave's arm.

"Look! There are Nancy and Ned! Nancy is writing something on a leaf."

The couple were too far away to distinguish

what it might be, but started to run forward as fast as they could over the mangrove roots.

When they reached the note, Bess and Dave read it quickly. *Going aboard. Couple one.*

"Going aboard what?" Dave asked.

He and Bess ran faster. A few moments later they saw Nancy and Ned hurry across the pier.

Bess exclaimed, "There's the sub! Oh my goodness, they're climbing down inside! We must stop them!"

Before the couple could get near enough to shout to their friends, they saw two men dash from the main building and get onto the submarine. Quickly they descended and closed the hatch. The ship submerged and took off.

Bess was in tears. "Oh, Dave, what's going to happen now to Nancy and Ned?"

Dave wasted no time in conversation. "Where's the office?"

"I'll show you," Bess said and the two sped off to the little building.

The door was open. Dave looked around for what he wanted to use, then began to send a radio message to the Coast Guard. In as few words as possible, he described what had taken place on Crocodile Island.

Within seconds a return message was received. Two Coast Guard cutters would be sent out at once. One would go directly to Crocodile Island. The other would go after the submarine.

"We will also send out two helicopters. Try to have someone tell them which direction the sub and the speedboat took," the Coast Guard operator said.

About this time the two policemen who had gone into the jungle returned. They were amazed to hear what had happened and thanked Dave for sending out the alarm. The officer had hardly finished speaking when they saw the two suspects being ushered into the area by George and Burt.

Patman and his companion looked astounded. "You caught them?"

George could not help quipping, "Yes, and with no guns!"

The officers gave the two prisoners a long look, then advised them of their rights to seek legal counsel. The two men exchanged worried glances but did not answer.

"Where does the sub go?" Patman asked. No reply.

Bess felt that treating the men gruffly was accomplishing nothing. She tried a softer, more kindly approach.

Smiling at them she said, "What about your families? Surely you care for them and would like to get back to them as soon as possible. You can't hide out forever."

One prisoner stared at her. "Are you some kind of preacher?" he asked. "You sure talk like one. But what you say makes good sense. I'll tell what

I know after Gimler and Sacco are caught. They
ran out on us, so I won't mind squealing."

Just then the group heard a motor and turned
to see the police launch coming. After it docked
and the two prisoners were taken aboard, the
officer in charge, Lieutenant Royce, said, *"The
Whisper* was spotted and the Coast Guard picked
up Gimler, Sacco, Carmen, and Tobin."

"Great!" said George. "But what about the
submarine? Two of our friends are prisoners
on it."

"A copter and two Coast Guard revenue cutters are after it," he replied. "They got directions
from Danny Cosgrove. He followed *The Whisper*
in the *Pirate*. The speedboat got away, but he
spotted the sub as it came out the channel. Danny
wigwagged signals to the copter. I'll see what else
I can find out."

He leaped ashore and went at once to the office.
In a few minutes he was back.

"Good news," the officer said. "Your friends
are safe and are on their way back. The smugglers
have been arrested. They wouldn't talk, but
Nancy Drew and Ned Nickerson told their story
for them, and for Gimler and Sacco. The freighter's captain is also in custody."

"Wonderful! Wonderful!" Bess cried out and
the whole group clapped. Bess, George, Burt, and
Dave hugged one another in their exuberance.

Lieutenant Royce smiled as he boarded the

launch and said, "Nancy, Ned, and Danny will meet you at the Cosgroves. A copter will pick you all up. Good-by!" He waved and gave orders to shove off.

In a short time the helicopter landed and soon Nancy's friends were back in Key Biscayne. There was a joyful reunion, and an exchange of stories far into the night.

Of course, Nancy, though happy at the successful outcome of the mystery, hoped another would soon come her way. It did. It was called *The Thirteenth Pearl.*

The following afternoon she and her friends went to see Mr. Gonzales in his hospital room. He was sitting up and declared he felt much better. "But let's not talk about me," he said, after Nancy introduced the others. "Tell me everything."

After he had heard all the details and thanked the young sleuths, Nancy said, "There's one question I have. When you told us not to come down here, was it because you were intimidated by Gimler and Sacco?"

"Yes," he admitted. "I see now why they didn't want you to investigate them." He smiled. "But I'm mighty glad you came. Thank you all for your superb work. And now," Mr. Gonzales said, "I have a surprise for you. I have taken over ownership of Crocodile Island. I want you to greet the new manager and his assistant."

He waved toward the corridor. Through the

doorway walked two smiling young men—Colombo and Sol! Nancy and the others cheered softly and congratulated them.

"Thank you," said Colombo. "And now Sol and I must get back to feed our pets, the crocodiles of Crocodile Island."

## Own the original 58 action-packed
# HARDY BOYS MYSTERY STORIES®
### In *hardcover* at your local bookseller OR
### Call 1-800-788-6262, and start your collection today!

## All books priced @ $5.99

| | | | | | |
|---|---|---|---|---|---|
| 1 | The Tower Treasure | 0-448-08901-7 | 32 | The Crisscross Shadow | 0-448-08932-7 |
| 2 | The House on the Cliff | 0-448-08902-5 | 33 | The Yellow Feather Mystery | 0-448-08933-5 |
| 3 | The Secret of the Old Mill | 0-448-08903-3 | 34 | The Hooded Hawk Mystery | 0-448-08934-3 |
| 4 | The Missing Chums | 0-448-08904-1 | 35 | The Clue in the Embers | 0-448-08935-1 |
| 5 | Hunting for Hidden Gold | 0-448-08905-X | 36 | The Secret of Pirates' Hill | 0-448-08936-X |
| 6 | The Shore Road Mystery | 0-448-08906-8 | 37 | The Ghost at Skeleton Rock | 0-448-08937-8 |
| 7 | The Secret of the Caves | 0-448-08907-6 | 38 | Mystery at Devil's Paw | 0-448-08938-6 |
| 8 | The Mystery of Cabin Island | 0-448-08908-4 | 39 | The Mystery of the Chinese Junk | 0-448-08939-4 |
| 9 | The Great Airport Mystery | 0-448-08909-2 | 40 | Mystery of the Desert Giant | 0-448-08940-8 |
| 10 | What Happened at Midnight | 0-448-08910-6 | 41 | The Clue of the Screeching Owl | 0-448-08941-6 |
| 11 | While the Clock Ticked | 0-448-08911-4 | 42 | The Viking Symbol Mystery | 0-448-08942-4 |
| 12 | Footprints Under the Window | 0-448-08912-2 | 43 | The Mystery of the Aztec Warrior | 0-448-08943-2 |
| 13 | The Mark on the Door | 0-448-08913-0 | 44 | The Haunted Fort | 0-448-08944-0 |
| 14 | The Hidden Harbor Mystery | 0-448-08914-9 | 45 | The Mystery of the Spiral Bridge | 0-448-08945-9 |
| 15 | The Sinister Signpost | 0-448-08915-7 | 46 | The Secret Agent on Flight 101 | 0-448-08946-7 |
| 16 | A Figure in Hiding | 0-448-08916-5 | 47 | Mystery of the Whale Tattoo | 0-448-08947-5 |
| 17 | The Secret Warning | 0-448-08917-3 | 48 | The Arctic Patrol Mystery | 0-448-08948-3 |
| 18 | The Twisted Claw | 0-448-08918-1 | 49 | The Bombay Boomerang | 0-448-08949-1 |
| 19 | The Disappearing Floor | 0-448-08919-X | 50 | Danger on Vampire Trail | 0-448-08950-5 |
| 20 | Mystery of the Flying Express | 0-448-08920-3 | 51 | The Masked Monkey | 0-448-08951-3 |
| 21 | The Clue of the Broken Blade | 0-448-08921-1 | 52 | The Shattered Helmet | 0-448-08952-1 |
| 22 | The Flickering Torch Mystery | 0-448-08922-X | 53 | The Clue of the Hissing Serpent | 0-448-08953-X |
| 23 | The Melted Coins | 0-448-08923-8 | 54 | The Mysterious Caravan | 0-448-08954-8 |
| 24 | The Short-Wave Mystery | 0-448-08924-6 | 55 | The Witchmaster's Key | 0-448-08955-6 |
| 25 | The Secret Panel | 0-448-08925-4 | 56 | The Jungle Pyramid | 0-448-08956-4 |
| 26 | The Phantom Freighter | 0-448-08926-2 | 57 | The Firebird Rocket | 0-448-08957-2 |
| 27 | The Secret of Skull Mountain | 0-448-08927-0 | 58 | The Sting of the Scorpion | 0-448-08958-0 |
| 28 | The Sign of the Crooked Arrow | 0-448-08928-9 | | | |
| 29 | The Secret of the Lost Tunnel | 0-448-08929-7 | | *Also available* | |
| 30 | The Wailing Siren Mystery | 0-448-08930-0 | | The Hardy Boys Detective Handbook | 0-448-01990-6 |
| 31 | The Secret of Wildcat Swamp | 0-448-08931-9 | | The Bobbsey Twins of Lakeport | 0-448-09071-6 |

### VISIT PENGUIN PUTNAM BOOKS FOR YOUNG READERS ONLINE:
### http://www.penguinputnam.com

### We accept Visa, Mastercard, and American Express.
### Call 1-800-788-6262